SYMPHONY OF BREATH

JO EDGAR-BAKER

EXPOSED PUBLISHING

Copyright © 2021 by Jo Edgar-Baker
Revised October 2022.
All rights reserved.
No part of this book may be reproduced in any form or by any electronic or mechanical means, including information storage and retrieval systems, without written permission from the author, except for the use of brief quotations in a book review.

So much gratitude to the priceless Dana Mitchell who helped me make this dream a reality.

*I dedicate this book to the gorgeous Theodore,
my beloved companion of 18 years.
You are my heart, and always will be.*

PART I

THE ENGLISHMAN AND THE GEISHA

THE ENGLISHMAN

LONDON 1874

Dwarfed by the traditional English desk he sat behind, Katsuhito bowed his head respectfully. "Mr. Montmorency. It brings me great satisfaction to have come to an arrangement."

"My family and I are honored," Ambrose replied, bowing lower to acknowledge the significance of the agreement they'd come to. He used the movement to discreetly slip the lucky medallion into his waistcoat pocket. It had worked its magic. The contract was finalized after months of negotiation.

"To celebrate our collaboration, will you join me for tea?" Katsuhito asked, bringing his fingertips together in front of his chin, as if blessing their partnership with a prayer. The Japanese businessman's face was relaxed in the closest approximation of a smile Ambrose had seen in the months they'd been in negotiations.

"I thank you, Katsuhito-san. It will be my pleasure."

Ambrose restricted his enthusiasm to a small smile. Along with much of the world, he had been ignorant of the culture of his host's homeland until recently, when Japan ventured into international commerce after more than two centuries of self-isolation. Both his inquiring nature and his professional association made him intensely curious about the customs he'd heard only whispers about. The opportunity to experience the solemn ritual with which the Japanese took tea was a valuable gift.

Katsuhito stood and moved to the door behind his desk. On the many occasions Ambrose had visited the Mayfair townhouse, he had been admitted only into the foyer and Katsuhito's traditionally furnished office. Had his host noticed his curious glances at the door which had always remained closed?

To Ambrose's surprise, Katsuhito removed his shoes. He then slid open the door and bowed in Ambrose's direction.

Holding his breath to contain his anticipation, Ambrose stood and hurried to join his host. He paused to remove his boots and place them beside Katsuhito's. The scent of jasmine and a distant tinkling of falling water welcomed him inside. Mimicking his host, Ambrose stepped through the portal, dipped his hands in a bowl of water, then shook out a small, rolled cloth to dry his hands. Only then did he glance around the room which would normally serve as a parlor, empty of all other furniture except a low table at its center. Intricately designed fabric in shades of gold, turquoise, and sea green reminiscent of the seaside hung on the walls. A sparse yet beautiful flower arrangement sat on the floor beneath a wall hanging with a Japanese symbol in black ink. Woven mats covered the floor, soft beneath his feet as he ventured after his host.

Cocooned by the atmosphere of tranquility and calm, it was difficult to imagine that the relentless cogs of the world's largest city ground on around them, and a maelstrom of humanity surged by just outside.

Katsuhito rang a sweet-chimed bell, then moved to kneel at the head the table, indicating Ambrose should do the same.

With some effort, the Englishman managed to fold his long legs beneath the table in a close approximation of his host and waited, breath held, for what would follow. As far as Ambrose understood, the tea ceremony was conducted by the host, or if in a tea house, by a geisha.

With a sigh, the door on the other side of the room opened and a woman entered. Ambrose noticed the fabric of her garment first. A kimono, he recalled from his frustrated attempts to learn everything he could about Japan. Lengths of rich fabric the color of midnight, scattered with ivory and gold dragonflies draped her small figure, held in place by a wide gold sash.

Ambrose was powerless to stop his gaze travel upward, drawn to her pale face. Her eyes were downcast as she seemingly floated toward the table, carrying a tray laden with cups and pots and implements. The sight of her stopped his breath.

She was even more exquisite than the fabric, with her glossy black hair arranged in an intricate style, her face powdered white, her brows elegant dark wings. And her lips! A bud of crimson blooming on her tiny, heart shaped face.

A geisha! Ambrose was astounded. He had never thought to be privileged to glimpse the most elusive of creatures. Katsuhito honored him indeed.

The details of the room around them blurred and Ambrose felt that he had been transported to an entirely different plane. It was more than her beauty that called to him. Despite her foreignness, he felt he *knew* her. When she glanced up at him, her appraisal fleeting as the brush of a feather, his stomach dropped as it did when he sometimes dreamed of falling.

Who *was* she? Why had she made such an impact on him—body, mind, and soul?

Whatever the case, she was to be respected, not stared at.

Politely averting his gaze, Ambrose studied the fine woodgrain of the table while he followed her movements in his peripheral vision. All his senses sharpened, homing in on her as she knelt and placed her tools and bowls just so. With a bow she placed a small plate in front of the two men.

"Wagashi wo Douzo," she murmured with a low bow.

"Please, eat. This is called *wagashi*," Katsuhito explained as he used the wooden pick to slice the small doughy ball. "It is made from sweetened boiled and mashed chestnuts."

Following Katsuhito's example, Ambrose sliced his *wagashi* and held a portion close to his nose before placing it in his mouth. He found the familiar scent of chestnuts and sugar combined with the unexpected rubbery texture on his tongue disorientating.

While he ate, Ambrose found himself captivated by the floating movement of the geisha's delicate hands, a form of meditation as she carefully cleaned her tools and began to make the tea. Each scoop of green powder was made with care, hot water added and whisked into a paste with the barest twist of her wrist, the pouring of the water onto the paste slow and deliberate.

"The tea ceremony originated in Zen Buddhism. It is traditionally made using seasonal fruit and nuts. Chestnuts represent autumn in Japan."

When he and Katsuhito both had a bowl of tea, Ambrose imitated his host, turning the bowl in his hands before lifting it to his lips with his palm held rigid beneath. The bitter earthiness of the tea was cleansing after the sweetness of the *wagashi*. Ambrose sipped again, savoring the exotic flavor.

Katsuhito bowed his head at the geisha. "Hisako. Will you play for us?" he asked quietly.

The silent geisha bent in an attitude of respect, then stood slowly before moving to the long wooden object at the far end of the room. She knelt behind it, sitting so she faced Katsuhito, and placed small, leaf-shaped objects over the ends of three fingers of one hand.

Hisako began to play, her body moving elegantly over the instrument as her fingers plucked the strings. The sweet melody drifted on the air like delicate blossoms. Ambrose breathed it in and was filled with peace. The haunting music transported him from bustling, dirty London to another land, a place of misty forests and sharp, rugged mountains. He longed to travel there and experience first-hand a culture where respect and serenity dictated the pace of life.

In contrast, the movement of her body and hands as she swayed over the instrument drew his gaze like a magnet, enlivening him with curiosity. Forgetting to show respect by looking elsewhere, his gaze lifted to her face. Despite the mask of white powder, and the red slash of her lips and eyelids, he could see by her expression that she was transported elsewhere, too. He willed her to, but not once did she glance up. How he longed to look into her eyes, to see the blush of her skin and lips uncovered...

Ambrose inhaled an unsteady breath and forced his gaze to the wall hangings. He must remember he was here on business. He must not disrespect Hisako or his host, and his father would expect a detailed description of the Japanese fabrics he saw.

He kept his eyes averted for the rest of the performance, and his ears tuned to each sound she crafted. In his mind he could see her every movement, could sense her every breath.

When she finished playing, a stillness settled over the room, the only sound the tinkling of water and his own breath, slow and deep. He had never experienced such a profound sense of peace.

The monotone of Katsuhito's voice broke into his trance.

"I wish you good evening, Mr. Montmorency. Thank you, Hisako. Would you escort our guest to the door?"

Ambrose stood and bowed low. "It has been an honor."

Katsuhito bowed but did not stand. "Please, will you

return next week? It is pleasing to have the company of one who respects our customs."

"Yes, of course." Ambrose flushed with pleasure. He hadn't expected to return so soon, believing his visits would end now that they had come to an agreement. The contract, jointly signed, would benefit both their countries. Japan would have British cotton to satisfy the demand they could not meet alone, and Britain's upper classes would have access to highly sought-after Japanese porcelain.

He felt the weight of his lucky medallion against his ribs. His family would expand their Manchester cloth business, and the months of Ambrose's residency in London was finally bearing fruit.

With a final bow of his head, he followed Hisako out of the room. She paused at the threshold of Katsuhito's study, waiting while he slid his boots back on, then led the way to the front door.

Ambrose was fascinated by the way she floated in front of him as if her feet were as unmoving as the rest of her body. He was unsure of the full duties of a geisha, although he was aware she held a very esteemed position, valued primarily for her conversation and knowledge of current affairs, and her skill at dance, music, and song. Katsuhito was a very lucky man indeed, having his own private entertainer living under his roof. But how did Hisako feel, owned by another person? The idea of it bewildered Ambrose. He knew that his countrymen kept and dealt in slaves, but his family never had. Did this life suit her? Was she happy?

Please look at me. Ambrose repeated the words in his head

like a mantra as they crossed the foyer. He yearned to see *her*, the spirit in the woman who wore a persona as carefully crafted as the physical trappings of her station.

She paused at the front door and turned to him to execute what he surmised was the Japanese equivalent of a curtsey. Then, as if she had heard his thoughts, she lifted her gaze to his.

The contact hit him like a blow. The red splashes at the outer edges of her dark lashes enhanced her mystique, while the beauty of her brown eyes—and what he sensed of her soul—took his breath.

Every woman Ambrose had ever met, including the beauties and the 'accomplished' gentlewomen from whom he was expected to choose a wife, paled in comparison to the diminutive foreigner standing before him. She was the most striking woman he had ever seen.

What did she think of him, a large, comparatively graceless stranger?

He longed to hear her voice, to have her speak to him, although he was certain it was forbidden.

Ambrose and Katsuhito continued to meet weekly to discuss business concerns in Katsuhito's study before they entered the tranquility of the tearoom. Ambrose lived for the moment he would see Hisako, hear her music, be in her presence. Apart from chasing down any lead available to learn more of Japan, including a music teacher who had some experience of Japanese musical instruments, he spent most days going through the motions of living. He dealt with business commitments like an automaton, yearning for Tuesday.

While Hisako quietly played her koto, the conversation gradually moved to more personal subjects such as family and childhood. While Ambrose watched the plectra—the delicate picks attached to three of her fingertips—dance across the strings, he learned that Katsuhito had a wife and children at home, although he did not expect to see them anytime soon.

Each week Ambrose was torn, dreading the time when he must leave Katsuhito's house and Hisako behind, while breathlessly awaiting the precious moments when she would show him to the door. For a short time, they would be gloriously alone. He learned to slow his breathing to prolong the experience, to absorb her presence through his senses. The barest rustle of fabric, the sound of her breath. The warm, exotic scent of jasmine. The enticing sight of the back of her neck where a delicious glimpse of flesh was bare of make-up.

All his senses—except touch—were filled with Hisako.

He longed to touch his fingertip to the vulnerable and naked skin and the curl of tiny hairs on her hairline. He yearned to reach out to her, to learn the silken texture of her hand, but knew it would be the gravest act of disrespect. Instead, he savored the priceless yet too brief gift of her gaze when she turned to say good-bye. For a moment he was privileged with a glimpse of the woman trapped inside a cocoon of costume and obligation, before he stepped back through the portal into the 'real' world.

After the peace inside, the reality of the street crashed over him. The bustle of pedestrians, carriages, and dogs was almost overwhelming. Here in Mayfair the stench of soot and sewage was less overpowering than other parts of London, yet it was bereft of the sweet scent of jasmine.

He longed to turn and step back inside. Somehow, the world of commerce and society he had lived all his life had become foreign to him.

Approaching the end of the fourth such visit, Katsuhito suggested Ambrose come later in the day next week and join him for dinner.

Ambrose arrived at the requested time, as the streetlamps were lit.

The meal was delicious, small portions of exquisite taste and presentation, served and cleared with the slow, deliberate hands of an older Japanese woman, yet Ambrose could not relax. Without the presence of Hisako, the room seemed cold and colorless.

When it seemed he could not process more new flavors, Hisako entered bearing a tray with the final dish. Ambrose took a deep breath, the muscles of his ribs easing with the familiar fragrance of jasmine and the sight of her graceful movements as she placed delicate glasses of frozen confections before the men. He waited until she knelt behind her koto and Katsuhito lifted his spoon before he scooped some of the flavored ice into his mouth. He closed his eyes in response to the angelic lightness, sweet and refreshing as Hisako's presence.

Rather than bowing her head to play, she plucked a few delicate notes and parted her lips.

With a growing sense of hopelessness, Ambrose held his breath, his ears tuned to the barest sound from her lips. When she sang, the delicate purity of her voice pierced his chest. His resolve melted as surely as the dessert on his tongue as her song grew, sweeter than any bird he'd ever heard. Spell-bound, Ambrose was unable to drag his gaze from her face, from her mouth and the glimpse of pink tongue. At one point, when he raised his eyes to hers and she looked back at him, he wondered that his heart did not burst from the emotion that blossomed in his chest.

In that moment, he knew he was lost. He needed her more than air to breathe, yearned for her more intensely than he'd ever wanted anything. But there was no chance for them. She belonged to Katsuhito, his business partner. She was bound by the honor of her family and her country, as Ambrose was bound to honor Katsuhito and their contract. What could Ambrose offer her anyway? Here, with her *danna*, she had everything she could need.

Except freedom.

Would she want it—would she want him—if her freedom was his to offer?

He knew it was impossible, yet he would die a happy man if he could just once experience the touch of her delicate hand on his cheek.

THE GEISHA

That night, after the Englishman took his leave, Mayumi was surprised to receive a message. She was wanted in the *danna's* room. Normally, he held her in such reverence he rarely asked her to perform the lovemaking arts. In fact, her amatory skills seemed to make him uncomfortable.

She removed her sleep gown and wrapped a simple kimono over her nakedness. Sexual pleasure was one of the many duties she had been rigorously trained to perform, and although the master would never force her to perform against her will, he *did* own her. Regardless, her master's unusual attention was not unwelcome. A restlessness had been swelling in her, a *need* she had been taught to dismiss. Spending hours so close to the light-haired, blue-eyed man, so full of energy and life, had woken in her a rebellious spark of self-indulgence. She had never felt so sensual as when she sang for him. His appreciation was almost tangible. She would have liked to imagine they were alone but did not dare forget Katsuhito was watching her every move, her every expression.

The only opportunity she'd had to drop her mask—for a few moments to be the woman Mayumi, not Hisako the servant—was when she escorted the Englishman to the street door. How she longed to leave with him, to walk out into the world beyond her luxurious cage.

Ambrose. She said his name in her mind as she walked the hallway to Katsuhito's room. She imagined the Englishman waiting for her. Pushing open the door, she found the *danna* where she expected him, kneeling at the foot of his futon in his *yukata*.

"My English friend wishes he could enjoy more of your company." Katsuhito's voice was rough with arousal, his gaze on her feet.

So, that was why he called her here. Jealousy had roused his possessiveness. He wished to re-establish his ownership.

Standing, he untied his robe and reclined on his futon, his gaze on the ceiling, his manhood rising insistent through the gap in the black fabric, ready for her to prove her loyalty, to show her obedience.

And she obeyed without question, unwrapping her kimono, letting it drop to the floor. In this life, especially so far from home, Mayumi had nothing but her training and her honor.

Katsuhito's gaze did not move from the ceiling, even as she stepped closer and straddled his hips. Even as she pleasured him, he did not look at her, closing his eyes as his arousal grew, trying to control his instinctive reactions. Yet his breath rasped and stuttered, beyond his control.

Frustration built inside Mayumi, even as her body clutched at the contact it craved, her pleasure spiraling high as it never had before. Mayumi yearned to cry out: *look at me! See me as a woman, not a possession, not a prized and precious object, too fragile to be embraced with lust. Hold me down, show me unrestrained passion! Take me by the hair, tug it while you kiss me deep and hard. If I must pleasure you, at least look at me like the Englishman does.*

She glanced down at Katsuhito, his lips pulled wide and thin in a grimace. Not once had she ever kissed him—nor any man. A pity, after all her training. So many hours practicing with the other *maiko* learning how to kiss a man on the mouth and drive him wild with desire. Is that why Katsuhito would never kiss her? Was he scared of losing control?

She closed her eyes and pushed him from her mind. He may own her body and dictate her behavior, but he would never control her thoughts.

Behind the darkness of her closed eyelids, she pictured the Englishman's mouth, easy to smile, lips firm and full. She imagined the softness of them beneath her fingertips, the hard pressure of them against her mouth as he pressed her back against the street door. She would wrap her legs around his hips as he thrust into her, his fingers pressing hard into her buttocks as her took her, rough in his desire. *Yes, yes...my Ambrose.*

My love.

THE ENGLISHMAN

After a restless night haunted by dreams woven from Hisako's song, Ambrose set off on foot in the direction of Mayfair with a roll of fine cloth over his shoulder as a gift for Katsuhito. He could not stay away, and justified his rashness with the need to thank Katsuhito for dinner in person.

With the phantom memory of Hisako's warm breath on his neck, her lips on his, he loped down the street, hoping the exertion of carrying the weight would blunt his urgency to see her. His plan was disappointed, his application of the door knocker fast and loud. Ambrose shook his head. What would the household think of his boorish behavior? What would the gentle Hisako think of him?

The older housemaid answered his knock. She bowed her gray-streaked head low, then led him to the tearoom via a different entry than the one through Katsuhito's office. Ambrose removed his boots and leaned the bolt of cloth against the wall before washing his hands and taking his usual place at the low table.

Hisako entered through her usual door, carrying the tea tray but dressed less elaborately than usual.

"Katsuhito-san is in a meeting," she said in a low voice, deeper than her song had led him to expect. How long had she practiced to master those light, high notes of her singing voice?

"I will make tea while you wait for him," she continued as she methodically arranged her bowls and tools on the low table, her words slightly halting but perfectly formed, her voice flowing through him like water. Water that could not quench his thirst for her; her words only increased his need for more. And so, he asked her questions while she made him tea, which she answered less demurely than he expected, her forthrightness at once giving him hope for her independence and dismay at the reality of her captivity.

"Your English is very good," he said, then realized how dimwitted he sounded. A geisha such as Hisako would be highly educated. In some ways, more so than he was himself.

"I speak four languages, although I have never spoken English with a native speaker." Her eyes sparkled, telling him she took pleasure in the experience.

"If you don't mind me asking, do you always take so much care with your hair and makeup and dress?" There was not enough time in the day—in his life—to ask her everything he wished to know about her and her experiences.

"Yes, every day. Sometimes more formally, although since

becoming *Geiko* I wear a wig. Before, my own hair was styled more elaborately, only once a week."

"How did you sleep?" he asked with wonder. Her appearance was always so smooth and perfect, how had she managed?

"With a special pillow," she replied with a secret smile, as if she knew giving him this small glimpse into her life would lead his imagination to forbidden places. "It is more of a wedge really, and supports the neck only, allowing the hairstyle to remain unspoiled."

"And every day you wear makeup?"

"Always. Unless Katsuhito-san is away on business."

How strange it must be, to always see the version of yourself dictated by another's ownership. Ambrose supposed it would be a constant reminder of her obligation. How often did Hisako see her true self? He wished she would reveal to him the face Katsuhito never saw.

Ambrose took the tea she offered him, bowing his head in thanks. He turned the bowl precisely and sipped.

Rather than her usual routine which would take her across the room to her koto, she remained seated next to him. She looked directly at him and began to sing, lightly at first. A song very different from the night before, her voice deeper and more natural as it grew in strength. To his ears, it sounded more sincere. More personal. Perhaps a song from her childhood?

Ambrose found himself being pulled into the story her tone and her eyes told. A story of yearning. He was entranced by the promise of her lips as they moved around the low, seductive cadence of her song. He leaned forward, the impulse to reach out to her so strong...

The knob on the door to Katsuhito's office rattled.

Hisako stopped singing, her face instantly blank. When Katsuhito entered from his office, she stood and bowed. Only when he had settled at the end of the table did she kneel again and begin the ceremony again to make them both tea.

"My apologies for visiting unannounced," Ambrose said. He paused, waited for Katsuhito's acknowledgement, then continued. "I have called today to thank you for a very pleasant evening, and to bring you a sample of a bolt of fabric, just arrived from our mill in Manchester." Nodding his head at the fabric leaning against the wall, he continued. "We have installed a new loom which allows us to produce an even finer weave than previously."

Katsuhito inclined his head and picked up his cup, turning it precisely in his hand before drinking. "Thank you for bringing the fabric. My clients are always pleased to see an increase in quality. I'm afraid I have a very busy day and have another appointment in a moment, so I must leave you with Hisako, who will see you out."

Not precisely a reprimand, but a dismissal that put Ambrose in his place. He was to visit only when invited. With a stiff bow, he turned to follow Hisako out of the room, his back tense.

The geisha's walk seemed less constrained than usual as she led Ambrose to the street door, her movements matching her less formal costume. *How would she act if she wore simple clothing, without the makeup of a geisha?* The imagining stole his breath.

Hisako retrieved his coat and hat. She held them out for him with her head bowed, turned to the side so she could see him from the corner of her eye.

She watched him as he did her. His ribs ached with the effort to not reach out and lift her chin. The sight of the bare skin of her neck, so close he could have bent to kiss the delicate wisps at her hairline, strained his willpower.

She dipped her head lower as she turned, and Ambrose fancied he felt the brush of her lips across the inside of his wrist.

Before he knew it, Ambrose stood out on the street, his hat and coat on. He looked down, stretching out his hand to find a small spot of red smeared on his skin, where his flesh still tingled. *Although forbidden, she had touched him!* Not only a caress, but from her lips.

He closed his eyes and pictured a similar smudge of red on his mouth, a dusting of her white face powder on his cheek. Ambrose turned to the solid black door, every part of him vibrating with the desire to push it open and pull Hisako to his chest. To carry her away and free her. But he could not. He was bound by duty to his family. He could not jeopardize the trade agreement he had brokered on their behalf.

Nor could he go home.

What should he do?

All he *could* do was appease his hunger to know her better, to satisfy his craving with any scrap or morsel available to him. Rather than turn for Bloomsbury, he walked in the direction of St James Square. He would go to the public library. They were constantly adding to their collection. Surely they would have something on Japanese geography and customs.

In the hushed dark rooms of the library he found only one volume, not comprehensive, but it was something. In it, Ambrose learned a little of the history, training, and different costumes of a geisha. He absorbed it like a starving man then wandered home in a haze, imagining Hisako's life. How strange she would find London if she were ever to escape her luxurious captivity.

The house he and his brother had leased was quiet when Ambrose finally returned. The aroma of meat, pastry, and gravy drew him through to the kitchen, his footsteps echoing through the empty townhouse. He silently thanked Armstrong, who had left him a plate on the range before she left to catch the last train to visit her sister.

His mouth watered as he collected a knife and fork from the benchtop. Not bothering with the formality of the dining room, he carried the plate to the kitchen table where the staff would have taken their meals. Except he didn't have staff, other than the housekeeper and a charwoman who came during the day to clean. Now Vincent was gone, off on his grand tour, it was just Ambrose and his daydreams in the Bloomsbury house.

Rolling up his shirtsleeves, Ambrose absently devoured the pie and potatoes, his mind full of Hisako. Was she satisfied in her position, or did she long to be free? Katsuhito was her *danna*, he owned her, but was she any less free than the average Englishwoman, with no rights except those her husband or her father allowed her?

Thirsty, he stood and went to the larder, looking for cider or ale. A flash of white caught his eye. A sack of cornstarch, pale as the makeup Hisako wore. Her cheeks and forehead were so smooth, what would it feel like to cup her face in his palm? Ambrose slid his fingers into the fine powder. He sucked in a sharp breath at the caress of cool silkiness against his skin. With the scent of jasmine filling his nostrils, he closed his eyes and cupped his fingers, imagining they held her delicate chin. He yearned to take her exquisite face in his hands, to cover her mouth with his, to taste her lips, luscious petals of red.

He was mad. He knew it, but he did not care. He was desperate for any reminder of *her*.

With a groan of frustration, he straightened and pulled his hand away. It came out as white as Hisako's face.

Ambrose closed his eyes and lay his palm, soft and silken, against his cheek. Imagining it was her smooth cheek pressed to his, he let out a shuddering sigh. He felt Hisako in his arms, her small hands in his hair. With a groan, he tipped his head back and dragged his fingers down his neck. His chest ached with frustrated yearning at the thought of her face pressed there, her mouth against his skin.

Ambrose clenched his fist, pressing it against his sternum. Every part of him yearned to run to her, to carry her away, but he could not. Compelled to act, he rushed from the kitchen. Instead of heading for the front door, he took the stairs, two at a time. He kept going past his bedroom, higher, up to the attic and his brother's studio. There was no lighting up there, just an oil lamp that he lit with shaking hands. Ambrose turned, sweeping the light across the bench.

As if Vincent had left just that morning, an array of brushes and paints that he'd not taken to Europe littered the surface. Ambrose scattered them, searching for a tube of pigment the color of Hisako's lips. *There.* A tube of red the color of poppies.

Dropping to his knees, he wrenched off the lid and squeezed a dollop onto his finger. Eyes closed and face raised to heaven, he smeared the paint across his mouth. If he valued his honor, this would be as close as he would ever get to kissing her lips.

The next Tuesday, Ambrose was unsure if he was expected at the Mayfair townhouse in the afternoon or evening. Or if he was expected at all. He had not heard from Katsuhito since his spontaneous visit the day after their dinner together. After Katsuhito's response on that occasion, Ambrose hesitated, but only for a moment. He could not wait any longer to see Hisako, so he dressed carefully and arrived in the afternoon, at the usual time for tea, his lucky medallion in his waistcoat pocket. Nike, goddess of Victory—he assumed that was the identity of the winged woman represented on the ancient, misshapen medallion a wise-woman had pressed on him in Athens—would surely help him now. *'Keep it close'* the Greek witch had urged him as she slipped it into his hand. *'If you have faith the gods will grant you that which you most desire.'*

At his knock, the elderly housemaid answered the door, then left him standing in the foyer. The house felt almost as vacant as his own. He could see that Katsuhito's office was empty through the open door. Had they all left, except for the housemaid? Uncomfortable with the feeling that he was intruding, Ambrose was about to let himself out when Hisako appeared on the landing above. Except this was not the Hisako he was accustomed to.

Ambrose's breath caught at the sight of her. With a sense of wonder, he took her in as she descended the stairs, from the small, bare feet peeking out from beneath a simple kimono of dove gray, to her hair, which was free of the elaborately styled wig. It hung in a simple braid over her shoulder. She wore no makeup.

He couldn't help but stare. *This* was the Hisako he had dreamed of, the woman he yearned to know. The geisha without her mask. His imagination could never have created a creature as stunning as the one who came to stand before him.

"I am sorry, Katsuhito-san is not here," she said.

"Oh?" Ambrose managed to reply, clasping his hands together. Her informal appearance and low, rich voice resonated with something deep inside him, making him want to abandon all etiquette.

"He has been called away on special business for his *daimyo*. Will you stay for tea?"

Ambrose touched his fingertips to the place where his

lucky medallion rested beneath his waistcoat and jacket. He could scarcely believe two of his greatest wishes had been granted, seeing Hisako like this, virtually alone. Ambrose was surprised. It must have been both unexpected and important. He would have thought the meticulous Japanese businessman would send a message to ensure Ambrose did not call by at the usual time.

"If it is not too much trouble?" he replied, his voice giving away his enthusiasm.

"Not at all. I am pleased to see you." There was no coquettishness in the look she gave him. Her gaze met his, her expression welcoming with a touch of uncertainty.

With a bow of her head, she showed him to a different room, smaller than the one where he and Katsuhito took tea.

Ambrose settled himself at the low table while she went to make her preparations.

He looked around while awaiting her return. The room was wood-paneled and warm, yet sparsely decorated apart from an elegant flower arrangement and a framed watercolor painting of dragonflies and watergrasses. Could this be Hisako's private living room? Ambrose had the distinct feeling he shouldn't be there, that he should not have seen her as she was.

When she returned with the tea tray and knelt across from him to make them both tea, he relaxed, comforted by her calm movements and the familiar routine.

"Will you tell me about your life, before?" he asked, beyond grateful for this unexpected opportunity to learn more about her, but anxious he was travelling down a forbidden path. What would the older woman tell Katsuhito?

"I grew up in a small village on the island of Shikoku. My parents were peasants and had very little. When I was six years old, they took me to the local *daimyo* and asked if he would recommend me to an *okiya*—a geisha house. Within a week I was taken to Kyoto and began my training. My name was Mayumi Tsuru then. Hisako is my geisha name."

"Mayumi," he repeated, drawing in a breath that filled him with a lightness he had never known. Her true name was the most precious gift on this day of wonders. *Mayumi.* The name of the woman he loved. Not the name of Katsuhito's geisha. "Are you glad, or would you have wanted to stay with your family?"

"I am glad. I have an education I would not have otherwise received. I have seen more of the world than very few other Japanese." She paused and looked at him, her lips parted on her quickening breath. "And I met you."

He smiled, joy surging through his body like a drug. He wanted to twirl and dance but held himself still. She was so calm and self-contained, he didn't want to scare her. *She cared about him!*

"I am very glad also," he said, his voice low with the strain of containing his elation and the powerful urge to protect her, to please her. To love her, body and soul. He leaned closer, longing to reach for her hand. *Did he dare to touch her?*

He yearned to ask if there could be more for them, but how could there be? She belonged to another. His family's business partner. The best he could hope for was to see her at times like this when Katsuhito was away. Would she want that? *Would it be enough?*

"Your training is very intensive," he said instead, schooling himself to calmness. "You play the koto and sing beautifully, *and* you speak four languages?"

"I am also knowledgeable on the subjects of politics, economics, and porcelain manufacture. I keep up with world events daily so I may hold a conversation on any current subject. And I dance," she added as if it was of little consequence.

Ambrose sat up straighter. He loved to dance but rarely came across a partner who possessed both light feet and a quick wit. "You dance?" he asked, breath quickening as he imagined the silk of her dove gray *obi* unfurling around them as he spun her in his arms.

THE GEISHA

"Would you like to see?" Mayumi asked, knowing that she should not. She was not permitted to perform for anyone without her *danna's* permission, but she could not stop herself. She sensed Ambrose would respond as Katsuhito never had, that he would appreciate the valuable skills borne of years of practice. Sometimes she wondered why she was taught so much when it was so little seen, and mostly by one man.

And she was right. At the beginning of the dance when she unfurled her fan, he tried to hide his fascination, to school his face to impassivity. By the time she knelt and placed the fan on the floor, looking him directly in the eye, he had turned to the side to watch her more intently, his expression openly entranced. Katsuhito never looked at her with admiration as a woman, only as a valuable possession.

She flushed with delight in response to Ambrose's enthusiastic clapping.

"I'm sorry, this is probably most inappropriate—if not unspeakably rude?" he asked, pausing with his hands not quite touching.

"It is. Very. But I like it." Joy bubbled through her. Her lips stretched into a wide smile, an expression that felt foreign on her face. She held still, willing him to come to her, to lift her to her feet and take her in his arms. To carry her out of this place and to his home. To his bed. She gasped at the force of her yearning, covering her mouth with both hands.

His gaze locked on her fingers, his pupils dilating so he looked not at all the civilized Englishman. He looked like the man she wanted him to be. The man who wanted to claim her, to ravish her as she never had been. Her breath came in pants, fingers brushing her lips as if she could tempt him to replace them with his lips.

"I am sorry," he exclaimed and hurriedly stood. "I must go. Thank you for a very pleasant afternoon." Pausing at the doorway to fumble his boots on, he hurried to the foyer where he collected his coat and hat himself. He did not stop to put them on before reaching for the front door.

Mayumi hurried after him. *Kiss me,* she almost whimpered, craving his embrace and the press of his lips on hers.

Kiss me! she wanted to cry out, desperate for him to know how much she wanted him. But she could not. A lifetime of training, of knowing her life was not her own, kept her mute. Those two words that represented her heart remained unformed on her tongue.

Yet, she could not let him leave!

"Katsuhito ordered me to send you a note telling you not

to come today!" Mayumi said quickly, reaching out to stop him. She froze and looked down at where her small hand grasped his much larger one. She gasped. His skin was so warm, so *alive*. She had convinced herself that touching his wrist with her lips the other day had been an accident, that she had overbalanced while handing him his coat. To touch a man other than her *danna* was forbidden. If Katsuhito saw them now, he could send her back to Japan, shamed and ruined.

But, whether he found out or not, she could not live the rest of her life without knowing what Ambrose's lips felt like.

THE ENGLISHMAN

Ambrose froze. He looked down at her small, pale hand on his, large and coarse by comparison. *She'd wanted him to come today so they could be alone!* With her words and that one touch of her hand he knew it was all over for him. He belonged to her, heart and soul.

The hairs lifted on the back of his neck as the realization sank into the very marrow of his bones. He had known for days that he was in love with Mayumi; he would be a fool not to. Now he knew the connection ran much deeper. Mayumi was the beat of his heart, the air he breathed. Their souls had been made to be together. He could not imagine a world without her.

An urgency he had never known engulfed him. He wanted to forget that they should not, that what he was about to do was unforgivable. Stronger even than his craving for Mayumi was his desire for her respect, but when she looked into his eyes, all he could see in her expression was his feelings for her reflected back at him.

Ambrose reined in his need, slowly reaching out to cradle her face. The gesture felt familiar. He had done this before, in his dreams, his fantasies, and yet the reality of touching her this intimately was pure ecstasy.

With a slow breath of sweet anticipation, he lowered his face to hers.

Her lips yielded to his, soft as petals, her breath mingled with his in a soft sigh. She moved close, sliding her fingers, featherlight, up his neck and over his scalp.

At the soft tug of her fingers on his hair, the hunger he'd held tightly in check roared to life. When the tip of her small tongue swept between his, inviting him to taste more, he dove in, kissing her deeply, as if by sharing oxygen they would become one.

He drew her closer, felt her lightness, delicate in his fevered embrace. Worried that his enthusiasm might hurt her, he took a shaky breath, took a step away, his hands on her upper arms their only physical connection. He could not let his baser instincts take control. As much as his body screamed for him to lift her up and take whatever she was willing to allow him.

She struggled, but not away. Rather, she moved with him, pressing her mouth to his, kissing him back, aggressive in her passion. She surged against him, like the tide climbing the shore.

Lord forgive him, he could not resist the feel of her so close, her breasts pressed against his chest, her thighs wrapping around his. He kissed her back with every ounce of the passion she ignited in him. If this was all they were to have, he would take this moment and brand it on his soul. He would live every day of his life with this kiss on his lips, and the impression of her body pressed against him.

The shattering of ceramics ricocheted in his head, bringing him back to reality with a crash.

Mayumi stiffened in his arms and they pulled apart, gasping as if surfacing from a deep dive in a cold pool. They both looked around, wide-eyed, but there was no-one to be seen. Mayumi slid down his body to the floor, her face almost as pale as when made up. Opening the door, she urged him to leave, squeezing his hand before closing the door in his face.

***

Ambrose could barely eat for worrying for Mayumi. Had they been seen, and by whom?

He did not send a note, for it might be read. He did not call by again, for surely if he went there, his uninvited appearance would only rouse suspicion.

Instead, he suffered the torture of uncertainty until the following Tuesday afternoon. With his lucky medallion clutched in his fist and hope in his heart, he set off for Mayfair.

When he arrived, it was as if he had dreamed their kiss. Everything was as it used to be in Katsuhito's house. Everything except Ambrose and the trajectory of his life.

The Japanese businessman welcomed Ambrose into his office, then regaled him with descriptions of the purchases he had made during his visit to Stoke on Trent. Machines that produced etched metal plates which could be used to create transfers to print onto ceramics rather than hand-painted designs. His *daimyo* had been very pleased when he had received an initial report of Katsuhito's discoveries, immediately organizing the transfer of funds for purchase of the technology. By adopting the transfer printing, his factories could significantly increase production.

In the months since their first meeting, Ambrose had never seen Katsuhito so animated. *Everything was not as it had been.* Could he hope that Mayumi's feelings for him had grown also?

"My *daimyo* is most pleased and has directed me to remain in London to seek out other relevant British innovations," Katsuhito announced with a satisfied expression on his normally reserved face.

"My congratulations," Ambrose said, bowing his head to hide the flare of joy that must surely show on his face. Surely this meant Mayumi would be staying also.

"Let us 'take tea,'" Katsuhito suggested, adopting the phrase of the country he would call home for the immediate future.

They arranged themselves at the low table as usual. Almost immediately Mayumi appeared. She was as graceful and tranquil as always, but there was no mistaking the hunger in her gaze when she glanced at Ambrose.

There *was* a tangible connection between them. Ambrose released the breath he'd been holding since the door slid open, then took a deep draft of the dizzying elixir of her regard. He looked away first, afraid their silent exchange would alert Katsuhito to their relationship—whatever it was or might be. He slumped under the weight of reality. What *could* it be? Mayumi belonged to the business partner of his family. Here or in Japan, she was lost to him, a prisoner of her circumstance. *Unless he could free her.*

Ambrose accepted a bowl of tea with a respectful bow. As much as he yearned to bask in her beauty and grace, he was careful not to look at her again. He need watch her to know her every movement, her every breath, as if it were his own.

Katsuhito was so buoyed by his recent success that he required little response from Ambrose, who could think of nothing but how he and Mayumi could be together. If that was what she truly wanted. If she just wanted to be free, he would help her find the life that pleased her. Even if it meant he was not a part of it, as much as that would pain him. If he was going to save Mayumi from servitude—to a man who cared nothing for her as a person but only as a status symbol and entertainment—he must have a plan.

By doing this he risked ruining both his personal and business reputation. It would mean turning his back on his duty to his family—to work in the family business, and to marry well and produce heirs for their growing dynasty.

It would be better if he and Mayumi left England for somewhere they could start with a fresh slate. The Americas, or Australia. His brother would have to step up and look after business in London instead of swanning around Europe painting landscapes.

He would walk away from it all if it meant he could be with Mayumi.

The rest of the visit passed in a blur of agitation. He longed to tell Mayumi his plan, but there was less chance of them being discovered if they left it to the last moment. Once he had the tickets and a date, he would tell her. In the meantime, he wanted to give her something to demonstrate his intention. A ring or a pendant would be ideal, but all he had with him was the medallion he'd slipped into the lower pocket of his waistcoat when he'd arrived. When she turned to him to hand him his coat, he pressed it into her hand.

Her eyes widened as she glanced at the misshapen metal disc in her palm.

As he shrugged into his overcoat, he looked down at the medallion against her pale skin and felt a sense of rightness. It occurred to him in that moment that the indistinct winged figure may well be Eros, the god of love.

Eyes glistening, she looked up at him and closed her fingers over the medallion. Raising her other hand, she opened her palm. A closed lotus blossom crafted of intricately folded red paper rested on her palm. She nodded her head, her expression urging him to take it.

As soon as he lifted the delicate flower from her hand, she gave him a quick smile and a curtsey then hurried away.

Out on the street, he slipped the flower into his pocket and hurried home. Only once he was inside did he take out the piece of origami, red as her lips. He groaned with desire. Gently, he unfolded the petals to reveal a single jasmine blossom, white and pure as the powder on her face and the connection he felt between their souls. Beneath the blossom was a tiny note.

Katsuhito will be away for one day and one night. If you want us to be together, we must go then. I will be ready.

Mayumi was already planning her escape to be with him!

With a jubilance he could barely contain, Ambrose sat down to write to his parents and his brother of his imminent departure from London. He then left for the docks to book a cabin on the next ship departing. Once they arrived at their destination, he would write to tell them more.

Their new home, he would leave to fate.

A week later.

Ambrose checked his watch and hurried out the door of his Bloomsbury house, barely able to comprehend the miracle that had befallen him. He was going to start a new life with Mayumi, a woman of seemingly infinite talent and beauty. She had chosen *him*, over the man who had given her everything.

The carriage ride to Mayfair, although measuring only minutes, felt like a lifetime, the reality of what he was about to do only making him more impatient for action. Ambrose's family had expected him to marry one of his own—a gentlewoman, reared to devote her time to charities and his household. Would they ever forgive him for stealing the forbidden, for running off to the colonies with a Japanese girl? Up in

Manchester, they had probably never heard of Japan, even though London had a small but growing population in residence.

Once they'd arrived at their destination, Ambrose approached the servants' entrance with unrestrainable excitement. *Mayumi.* Her name was a tattoo in his mind, hurrying his steps. His very blood pulsed with yearning for the moment they would be free of London.

Everything was in place. He'd received word from the housemaid who was sympathetic to Mayumi's situation. A middle-aged woman, she felt a motherly concern for her young companion's happiness and had agreed to help her escape when the master was away tending to business in Staffordshire. She would be waiting for his knock.

But it was not the housemaid who answered the door.

It was the *danna* himself.

Katsuhito said nothing, but stood solid in the doorway. There was no mistaking the anger radiating off him, despite his stillness. His face, once softened in friendship and respect, wore a stiff mask of disdain.

"Katsuhito-san," Ambrose rasped out as he took a step back.

"This is how you repay my hospitality? The respect I have shown you as a business partner. As a friend." Ambrose had never heard the guttural, clipped tone from his host before. With a sinking heart, he realized how dire the situation was.

"We are in love," Ambrose said, by way of explanation. To him, it was all that mattered.

"Love?" he sneered. "So, you thought you could steal my

property? I *own* Hisako. If she does not love me, she may love no-one."

"Her name is Mayumi," Ambrose insisted stubbornly. Then a horrible thought occurred to him, and the sick feeling he had ignored all morning rose up to engulf him. "Is she well?"

"I have not harmed her if that is what you imply. I will not set eyes on her again. She is gone—returned to Japan with the greatest dishonor. No longer geisha. Her only option will be to live as a whore." Katsuhito's mask shattered, the hurt and anger of betrayal twisting his expression, making his sharp, high cheekbones sharper still. His warm skin turned pale and cool. Ambrose reached out toward him, wondering if he was about to be sick. Or keel over.

Katsuhito stepped out of Ambrose's reach and spat noisily on the ground beside his feet. "Our partnership is over. Your fantasy is over. She is gone," Katsuhito barked as he turned and slammed the door.

Stumbling back onto the street, Ambrose paused. He spun around, running an agitated hand through his hair, his feverish need for activity seeking an outlet. What could he do, where should he go?

A seed of hope sprouted amidst his despair. *He would search the wharves.* Maybe the ship she was traveling on had not yet departed. And if it had, he would find another ship, or series of ships, that would take him to Japan. He would find her and save her from the life of shame Katsuhito had condemned her to—all because of him. A sense of purpose filled him with renewed hope. They would be together after all!

I will find you! Ambrose promised her as he turned back to the waiting carriage. His steps faltered at the teasing drift of jasmine on the breeze. A small hand grasped his arm. *Mayumi!* He swung around, hope surging through him, making him dizzy with its intensity.

But it was not the precious face of his Mayumi. It was the older housemaid, her eyes wet, face puffy from crying.

The old woman placed something in his hand and looked up at him. "I am...sorry. I told." She paused, as if she had run out of words that were foreign to her.

"Your master?" Ambrose finished for her, feeling sick. She had seen them. The breaking ceramic. It was her. She had betrayed Mayumi.

The woman nodded with a sob, then turned and shuffled back to the house, head and back bent.

Ambrose opened his palm. Three ivory plectra lay in his glove. How often had he seen these picks secured to the tips of Mayumi's delicate fingers as she knelt gracefully playing her beloved koto?

She had left them for him. But what would she use to play her beloved koto? Did she have more, and what of her instrument?

His fingers curled over the plectra, taking care not to crush them. His eyes felt as though they were burning in his head. Had Katsuhito taken that from her too?

THE PARTING

Her hands finally freed, Mayumi ran out onto the deck, barefoot and wearing only the gown she had been sleeping in when she'd been taken from her bedroom. She shivered and rubbed her wrists, inhaling the frigid, salt-laden air, trying to cleanse the stench of the oaf who had manhandled her first into a carriage, and then onto the ship, tying her to the bed in a tiny, windowless cabin.

Clasping Ambrose's medallion in her fist, she sagged against the rail at the sight of the riverbank gliding past. The combined weight of Yui's betrayal, Katsuhito's vicious reaction, and the anguish of not being there when Ambrose came for her, crushed the air from her body.

Her body, frozen with dread, swayed with the rising waves as the ship moved farther down the river, the growing roar of the breakers calling the vessel out to the ocean that would carry her away from Ambrose, away from all hope of happiness.

She would not—could not—leave him, her heart and soul. There was nothing for her in her homeland but shame and failure.

With his medallion clutched tight in her hand, she climbed onto the rail. There, she balanced for a moment, suspended between sky and water, past and future, joy and despair.

No, she would not be taken from him.

Spreading her arms like the outstretched wings of the woman on the medallion, she lifted her face to the damp gusts…and tipped forward. For a few precious moments her spirit soared as her body flew into the unknown.

Ambrose my love, I will find you again.

Mayumi Tsuru. Ambrose found the name of his heart's greatest desire listed on the manifest of a ship which had already departed.

As Katsuhito said, she was geisha no longer.

Without delay, Ambrose organized to travel to Japan with the next cargo of his family's cotton. He telegraphed his father to inform them he was relocating to secure more business, and that his brother Vincent should return from Europe to take his place as the company representative in London.

In Japan, after his enquiries yielded no information, Ambrose integrated as best he could. Duty-bound to compensate his family for neglecting his commitments in

London, he established an office in Kyoto and slowly built trade for his family's business. Everything else he did was to find Mayumi. He searched every geisha house and brothel, torn between relief and despair every time he was told she was not there. With each year that passed, he despaired of the shame and degradation of the life meeting him had condemned her to.

He located her family, but they had not heard from her since she visited before she left for London. For all his efforts and dedication, he did not find Mayumi.

At the age of thirty-eight, Ambrose contracted the new, more virulent form of cholera, *mikka korori*—or three-day drop-dead.

The irony was not lost on Ambrose. The epidemic was believed to have been introduced by American sailors after Japanese ports and trade were re-opened to the world. Trade had led him to his love, and trade would cause his death.

"Mayumi," he gasped through parched lips.

"I will find you," he promised with his last breath, scented with jasmine.

PART II

THE COMPOSER, HIS MUSE AND HER SISTER

JASMINE

LONDON 1998

The fabric of my dress swirls and flaps against my legs, driven by gusts of moist air heavy with salt residue. Beneath my feet, the deck surges, the dark waters of the Thames parting, churning along the hull. Above, the sky is an infinite dome of blue.

I feel at once insignificant, yet also somehow an integral thread in this great city's existence. A strange feeling, after spending only a fraction of my twenty-five years in London, to feel such an instant connection. Is it possible to experience love at first sight with a place?

After months of touring, being out on the water is like waking up in an alternate universe. An abrupt change of gear after months of nights in smoky clubs or concert halls and days on the road, to fresh salty air and sun on my skin. Strangely I feel a sense of loss. For the end of the tour? I know I will miss London, but I should be excited to go home at last. Back to Australia with its vibrant light and upside down seasons. Back to my family.

The rest of the band have chosen to stay on dry land and sleep in, but I don't want to miss a moment of my last days here. I'm going to experience all I can of this strangely familiar city.

Most of my fellow passengers are crowded in the bow, waiting for their turn to spread their arms and pretend to be Kate or Leonardo in *Titanic*. I close my eyes and tighten my hands on the rail, listening to the sounds of the river, the rhythm of the splash of waves, savoring the moment, precious for being so rare and fleeting.

Spending time by myself always sparks my creativity. I can already hear the beginnings of something new—something different, yet strangely *known*—growing in my soul. The teasing melody of a new composition. New, but with the haunting familiarity of a long-forgotten melody from childhood, or some element of my Japanese heritage I thought I'd missed out on growing up with my adoptive Australian family.

With my feet rooted to the deck, my body moving with the boat through wind and waves, the composition strengthens and grows. I open my eyes, my gaze drawn to the water below, which seems to be speaking to me.

My fingers itch for my old violin, untouched for almost a decade, carefully stored back in my room on the farm, protected from extremes of temperature, strings loosened. I hadn't thought about her for so long, but suddenly I yearn to hold my old friend again, to make her sing. Instead, I slip my hand into the pocket of my dress and grasp the medallion I'd bought from a stall of mud lark treasures this morning. The coin had called to me and I didn't resist. It wasn't the traditional souvenir I'd had in mind when I visited the market, but to me it represented what I most loved about London. The history. The mystery. Even now I can make out the figures moving along the banks of the river looking for treasure amongst the rocks and mud. How long had the misshapen medallion been hidden in the silt of the Thames before it was found? A year or a century?

I close my eyes, the slight weight of the warm metal comforting in my hand. Which god or goddess did the rudimentary figure stamped into the metal represent? I search my knowledge of mythology. The artwork is simple, it could be male or female, although the wings are obvious. It could be Fortuna, goddess of fortune, or Mercury, god of travelers that called to me.

My blood thrums with exhilaration as a gracefully fluid melody takes form in my mind. The notes start softly, gentle as the seagulls riding the thermals, swirling around the sails. Building and rising as the waves rush against the boat, pressing against the planks of the hull. The tempo grows and swells until the joy of it almost bursts from my chest.

Yes. I feel like calling out with elation, my spirit soaring. If I can encapsulate these feelings, the loss and joy, the past and future, I might create something truly great and memorable.

Where to next? The melody should reflect the agonies

and ecstasies of life, a foreboding decline before the ultimate lift to enlightenment. And how to weave all the elements into a satisfying end?

Thoughts of home and being with my family evaporate, overtaken by the sudden and overwhelming desire to hear the composition complete, to glimpse the source of its beauty.

I search the surface of the river, my gaze plunging beneath the waves, reaching for inspiration. If the creatures of the sky, the air itself, have spawned this epiphany, what answers might I find beneath the water?

I see myself reflected on the surface, my dress flapping behind me like wings. I search the flickering depths, grasping after shadows of midnight blue and turquoise that flash and flee. A haunting refrain floats through my mind. I feel the echoes in my blood, the sounds of my heritage in the traditional instruments of Japan merging with the classical training that has become part of my soul.

A pair of blue eyes rise out of the darkness. Beautiful, beloved eyes. A spasm of need pulls at my heart, so strong that I gasp with the unexpected shock of it. I lean closer for a clearer look, gripping the rail.

The ship rises, cresting a freak wave, the sudden surge rendering me weightless. My feet leave the deck, and I am flying, the salt breeze lifting and caressing, my heart soaring with freedom and the promise of joy. I can hear it now, the final bars of my composition, as my vision fills with the sight of *him*, arms open, waiting to catch me.

I will find you. His words echo in my mind.

I am encircled in his embrace. I curl into him. Music fills me, the end of the composition buoying my soul even as I plunge beneath the waves. An answer to the loneliness that has haunted me for a lifetime.

Finally, I am home.

THE COMPOSER

LONDON 1913

For a moment, the notes—and the music—cease to make sense. The ones he has written *and* the ones that float just beyond his grasp. With a frustrated sigh, Archibald looks around his workroom as if he has never seen it before. Even the familiar paneled wood walls and empty hearth seem as two-dimensional as a newsreel projected on a cinema screen.

He must finish!

The completion of the symphony is the only thing that keeps him from the oblivion he so longs for: his only remaining earthly tie—the opening night dedication on the anniversary of his son's death.

He was unable to delay the orchestra further than next week. Any longer and there is no way they will be ready to perform his new symphony as planned.

Panic rises in his chest to clutch at his throat. For a

moment, he is helpless in the face of the anguish that accompanies the thought of failure.

With a deep breath and force of will, he unclenches his hands before he damages his precious violin. The memories are too close, too raw, here in the home where he still sees Benjamin in every room. Not even the weight of the violin in his hands can steer him closer to the music he needs to create.

Frustration translating into movement, he stands, the sudden movement tipping his favorite music chair onto its back.

It is no use. The missing piece that will make sense of years of toil eludes him. The last movement of his symphony that must weave together the joy and the excruciating pain is no clearer today than it was that devastating day ten months ago.

'Les Modes de Vie'. The Ways of Life. A testament to his son's life—and his death. Even now, the pain of losing Benjamin, and the sense of drifting since his wife abandoned their union, is no easier to bear.

With reverence and regret, Archibald packs away his instrument and descends to the kitchen. The meditative ritual of making tea, inhaling the fragrant steam and savoring the exotic taste, usually calms him, opening his mind to creativity. For once the matcha he first tasted at the Japan-British exhibition with Benjamin fails to relax him. Restless, he picks up the ancient coin from the center of the table where he dropped it yesterday. He'd accepted the oddly shaped medallion as payment from a laborer for his daughter's music lesson. No child with talent should be deprived of tutelage, and the coin interested him. Jones said he'd found it when he'd worked on the Greenwich foot tunnel, dug from the earth beneath the Thames.

Archibald stands. It is no use. He will achieve nothing here today. His only hope is to distance himself from the ghosts of his failures, to seek the familiar comfort of his old piano and studio at the school where he first learned to tame his talent.

Leaving the cup on the table, he shrugs into his coat, dropping the coin in the pocket. If he were a hopeful man, he might believe the crude depiction of a winged woman represented his muse, coming into his life when he most needed her help to honor his son with his greatest work.

It is cold out, but there is only one place he can think of that inspires him when all else fails: his favorite detour on the way to the station. Each step on the path through the botanic gardens, past the Gateway of the Imperial Messenger, helps to blunt the ragged edges of his grief. An echo of his son is here, in the elegant lines of the replica Japanese temple they first saw together at the Japan-British exhibition before he became ill. While Archibald was entranced by the traditional Japanese music, his son had fallen in love with the gardens—the plants, bridges, even the rocks, brought all the way from that mysterious country.

Meningitis stole Benjamin away before the temple was re-assembled in the Kew Gardens close to their home, where he could have visited every day if he'd wished.

Archibald hunches his shoulders against the strengthening wind and plunges his hands deep in his pockets, his fingers bumping against the hard, rounded edges of the coin. He inhales deeply to ease the sudden constriction of his chest, then freezes, mid-breath. He knows the scent of jasmine is in his imagination. It is too cold now for the plant to flower, but the scent lingers as a ghost of those happy days with his son, reminding him of Benjamin's impatience to leave the confines of the tea house to explore while Archibald stood transfixed with wonder at the sight of the foreign musicians. He can still clearly picture the brightly robed woman, kneeling to play a Japanese stringed instrument, accompanied by a man playing a bamboo flute. A comforting sense of déjà vu had held Archibald there until the performance was finished, the musicians departed.

Standing now at the foot of the temple, he hears the echoes of music in his mind. Could this be what he needs to link the unfinished pieces of music into the symphony he has promised? The string and wind instruments—the koto and shakuhachi—were amongst the items donated to the British public after the exhibition. But he does not have time to find them, or someone who knows how to play them.

The mournful notes of the Japanese music follow him to the station and beyond, teasing him, echoing in the surge of the train along the tracks as he travels to his old school. There, he *will* find the clarity to move forward. The ancient piano where he composed his first pieces as a student—the instrument that reminds him of every success—is his best hope to unlock his creativity and finish this symphony, his ninth. For two hours he tries, in the familiar embrace of the music room. His private studio until classes resume in two weeks.

As a storm forms and rages outside, he plays through the first three movements, hoping the finale will grow and bloom like the cherry blossoms Benjamin had so admired. He needs *something* to tie those elements of the first three movements together. All that comes is the anguished grief that constantly gnaws at him. He has become a shell of himself. He would never have admitted it, but Archibald once suspected he loved his music and his only child equally, the two joys of his life. Now he knows better. Without Benjamin there *is* no joy. The only reason he keeps going is to commemorate his son's life.

Shivering with cold and hopelessness, he shrugs on his coat. Dropping his head in his hands, Archibald doesn't even have the energy to sob. It is hopeless.

Gradually, an awareness pulls him out of the dark cavern inside. A presence, close by. Benjamin, come to visit in spirit, to give him the strength to continue? Archibald never believed in seances or the afterlife, not until Benjamin was taken.

When he looks up, his heart in his throat, it is not a boy of twelve Archibald sees, but the shimmering vision of a tall, slim woman with dark hair in pale blue dress. For a moment she seems almost solid as a person, standing by the window. He holds his breath, not daring to blink, and she shimmers there until the sun comes out from behind the clouds, the sudden light flaring in his vision.

And she is gone.

Archibald closes his eyes and sees an echo of her features in his mind. She seems familiar, but from where? Was the vision the ghost of a memory or a figment of his unstable imagination? Or *was* she a ghost?

Out of the blue, notes from his symphony float through his mind. His fingers twitch. The echo of the Japanese instruments from the exhibition rise in his consciousness, weaving amongst the elements of his symphony. He returns to the piano, his fingertips hovering over the keys. Tentatively at first, he plays the notes to accompany the music in his mind, a melody glimmering with hope.

His heart beats fast with excitement. This familiar yet foreign ingredient is the answer, an exotic taste to a jaded tongue. Those memories of that special time he and Benjamin spent together, told with sound, are the way to honor his son.

He works on. Tender with love, the composition remains insubstantial as sunlight, elusive as a rainbow.

He looks up in the direction of the window, hoping to see her—his muse—come again to help him move forward. She has not. Although he perseveres, exploring the fragments of music she gifted to him, the notes roll over themselves, victims of his fatigue.

He can go no further today.

The next day Archibald wakes with purpose and sets off early with the muse's coin in his waistcoat pocket. He hurries back to the school where he spent much of his youth and many hours since as a teacher, praying she will come to him again. And come she does, but not in the classroom.

As he steps out of the station building, about to hurry in the direction of the school, a fleeting flash of her blue dress beckons him. He dashes to catch up. When she disappears around a corner, he follows. He loses sight of her, slows to search for a glimpse of blue fabric and long dark hair… catches a glimpse, hurries forward. For the first time in almost a year, he finds himself smiling. She teases him, just as she teases the music from his soul.

He continues, his pace quickening until he finds himself at the river's edge. Looking around, he realizes he has walked as far as Greenwich. He glances up at the wide blue sky and breathes deep. Here, with the direction of the breeze from the sea, the odors of the city are less offensive.

Gulls wheel around him, riding the thermals, and the sun caresses his face with its weak rays. He takes a breath of salt-laden air, with a hint of the elusive scent of jasmine. He pauses and certainty fills him with strength. Now he has found his muse, he will finish his symphony.

Returning to the school, Archibald takes a seat at the piano. He starts to play, pausing regularly to record his work. He recalls the path his muse led him on and the feeling of hope and freedom he found at the edge of the river; how close she felt, as if, if he plunged into the surging water, he would find her there. The loss of his son is still a constant ache, a missing piece of his soul, but he finds glimmers of joy in the memories, which filters now into the music he creates.

Each morning he leaves home with a new energy,

knowing he will find her on the way. Even when he cannot see her, he knows by the warmth on his skin and the fragrance in the air when his muse is with him. Her presence gives him strength and hope.

Each day that he sits at the piano brings him another step closer to fulfilling his goal—to honor his son's short life.

THE MUSE'S SISTER

LONDON 1998

Jetlagged and befuddled, Olivia hurried from the hospital reception, Jasmine's favorite childhood toy clutched to her chest. Down the hallway she'd been directed to, she searched the room numbers, oblivious to the sting of antiseptic in her nostrils, blind to the green-clad doctors and patients she passed.

20C, 20D.

I'm coming... she called out to her sister in her mind.

20F. Stopping abruptly, Olivia gathered herself before peering through the glass panel of the door. And stiffened in shock.

Jessie? Surely that was not her sister's long dark hair almost entirely hidden by bandages, her lovely skin pale against her blue gown and white sheets. It could not be her vibrant, strong sister lying there unmoving and vulnerable. Olivia's grip tightened on the plush toy koala. It felt like her only connection to reality.

The nurse turned, as if sensing her presence, and beckoned her inside with a wave of her hand.

"Relative?" she asked as Olivia stepped inside, her gaze raking the prone body in the bed.

"Sister," she choked out, after registering the familiar chicken pox scar on her right cheek.

"Oh, Olivia? All the way from Australia. You got here fast."

"As fast as I could. How is she?"

"Doctor will be around soon. She'll be able to tell you more, but your sister bumped her head when she fell from the boat. She's in a coma. Depending on what you believe, she might be able to sense that you're here. If you want to sit with her, talk to her while you wait."

"Yes, of course." Olivia pulled the chair to her sister's side and snuggled the soft body of her koala into the crook of her arm. The arm that had the least number of tubes and wires attached to it.

"I brought Koto," Olivia explained to Jessie, falling back into the tone she'd used to reassure the shy, young orphan her parents had brought home nineteen years ago. *Her new sister.*

"It was the first time he'd flown so he was a bit nervous, but he was so excited to come and see you." Olivia's voice fractured. The words sounded silly to her ears, but what did one say to their younger sister when she was balanced on the brink of death? *What the hell were you thinking?*

Olivia shook her head, tears of anguish and frustration washing her cheeks. How was it possible to fall from a boat with rails to protect you—unless you were doing something stupid? And Jessie never did anything stupid. Daring, maybe, but risks always paid off for her sister, the gifted one.

"I've missed you," she sighed, her shoulders sagging. Just last week they'd spoken on the phone, discussing all the things they were going to do when Jessie came home.

It wasn't fair. She had seen so little of her sister these last eight years, with Jessie's escalated study at the conservatorium in Brisbane, then the tours. Now, just when they were about to have some quality time together...

Olivia clenched her fingers in the crisp hospital sheets. She wanted to throw something, to scream at the unfairness of life. But that wouldn't help her sister. She had to be the strong one now, and be here when Jessie came out of it. Olivia would make her favorite meal, and then they would spend time together, laugh, and gossip like old times.

THE COMPOSER

LONDON 1913

Despite his impatience to continue work on the symphony, on the sixth day Archibald finds his morning taken up attending to outstanding accounts his wife would normally have dealt with.

Today, his muse does not appear to him on the way to his studio at the school.

At the piano, he feels unsettled by her absence and cannot progress past a dark and angry interlude. After hours of frustration, he trudges home, studying every figure he passes, every shadow, desperate for even glimpse of her. He needs her presence to finish.

But there is nothing but gray and black and a premature darkening of the sky.

Back at home, he sits in his library. But even with his violin in his hands, making music seems impossible. The comforting weight that would normally bring him some small measure of peace, is heavy with expectation and potential disappointment. He has only one day to finish before he must present the work to the conductor.

Archibald stands, tossing the violin onto his armchair, his frustration and disappointment heating to anger. Anger at himself for announcing too early that the symphony was almost completed, for too hastily booking musicians and the hall for rehearsals. Anger at his muse for deserting him when he needs her most. Anger at the disease that took his son and broke his wife.

It is no use. Here, or at his old schoolroom, he will not finish in time. Resolved, Archibald stalks to his bedroom and seeks out what remains of the bottle of oblivion that his wife used to dull her pain after Benjamin left them. Then, Archibald had been determined to do the one thing he could think of for Benjamin–be strong for his inconsolable mother. Now, in his dejection, he doesn't bother to measure the poppy juice. He tosses the bitter liquid back, uncaring if the dose is too much, almost hoping…

Pulling on his dressing gown, he returns to the library and drops into the chair where his son once sat. He longs for the days when Benjamin used to sit there, enthusiasm lighting his precious face as he asked for another song, for more silly lyrics. Where had that Archibald Flagstaff gone? The playful man, eager to act the fool for a smile and a giggle from his beloved boy?

The opium creeps through his veins, the room around him wavering as if underwater. In the shadows of the corner, a vague form materializes. His son? He tries to sit forward but has become one with the cushions.

A flash of pale blue fabric, a ripple of long hair, a teasing smile, a pair of lively brown eyes. *His muse?* The figure takes on a more solid appearance, her dark hair now pinned up. Her features resemble his muse, but it is not her. Her face is pale as a winding sheet, her lips blood red. Two different women, *with the same vibrant brown eyes.*

The woman with him now in some ways resembles the musician who played the koto at the Japanese exhibition, but it is not her. His companion is more delicate, her slender neck as graceful as her movements as she bows her head to pluck a haunting melody from the strings.

He leans forward, her music releasing him from his paralysis. The notes creep through him on the back of the drug, infusing his heart and permeating his brain. The sound from the instrument is different in style and execution from the exhibition, the musician infinitely more gifted.

His muse glances up at him from crimson-smudged eyes. In that instant he knows for certain he is not reliving a memory from this life. She is from a different plane, another past. An exquisite creature dressed in midnight and gold, a doll come to life, her pale face in stark contrast to her dark hair, elaborately styled, her lips red as blood. *Lips he longs to kiss.* Eyes that *see* him, a different version of himself that *has* kissed her. A slap of recognition sends him reeling backward. He knows this woman. Intimately. He loves her...

Mayumi. The name comes to him as if floating on the air.

She stands, suddenly bare of makeup, so strikingly beautiful the sight of her stops his breath, her warm skin so smooth he yearns to touch it. Her music fills him, filling the cavity in his soul and lifting his spirit. Joy releases him from restraints of social convention. Here stands his muse, *his music*, why should he not reach for her?

Her lips part. Deep in his soul he knows she wants to kiss him. Wants him to kiss her. He *will* kiss her, but for a moment he hesitates, savoring the moments before their lips meet. She is so close he breathes her breath, as she breathes his. Their lungs move in opposition, one breath complementing the other, both tied to the music. *A symphony of breath.*

The anticipation is dizzying, his soul swooping and soaring in time with his music—the music she brought to him.

He has been waiting for her, as she has waited for him, for more than a lifetime.

When he can resist no longer, he lowers his head the small distance to press his lips to hers...

His connection with his life splinters. For a moment he holds the woman he searched for for so long, before she is torn from him, pulled beneath water. All he sees is her deathly still, draped in pale blue cloth, his muse, the woman who has been haunting him.

Then vibrantly alive, dressed in midnight and gold. Melting against him.

"Where are you? You said you would find me." Her voice sobers him for a moment.

Yes. He must find her. Whatever he has to do.

Reason deserts him as the full force of the drug takes hold of his body and his mind, and pulls him under...

THE MUSE'S SISTER

LONDON 1998

Each day Olivia sat by sister's hospital bed, talking to her, reliving every good memory she was able to recall. When she wasn't at Jasmine's side, she wrote down any newly uncovered memory so she could share it with her sister the next day.

Each day Olivia became more desperate to find that one memory that would pierce Jasmine's consciousness and bring her back, knowing that the longer her sister was unconscious, the greater the chance she would lose her forever.

Eventually, Olivia ran out of memories. For lack of a better idea, she brought in her Discman, with a speaker she purchased from a shop down the street. The few CDs she'd brought with her from Australia were mainly pop music, but she was desperate.

"I hear classical music can be therapeutic," one of the nurses suggested. "And calming," she added, looking pointedly at Olivia's ragged fingernails and puffy eyes. "There's a library a block away. They have shelves of CDs. I'm sure you'll find something you'd like to borrow."

When Olivia stepped out for food, coffee, and air that wasn't recirculated, she followed the signs to the library without a second thought. Stepping inside, she sank into its quiet, calm tranquility.

The guy at the desk looked up with a smile. He was handsome in an outdoorsy, ruddy sort of way. Normally her lack of self-confidence would have had her searching out another staff member, a woman or a less-attractive man. Olivia stepped forward. At home, everyone knew her as the beautiful and brilliant Jasmine Thompson's plain older sister, but nobody knew her in London. She was only here for music for her sister, after all, not a date.

"One of the nurses at the hospital suggested I borrow some CDs." Olivia stumbled a little over the words. The gentle look in the attendant's gray eyes encouraged her to go on. "To play for my sister. She's in a coma."

"I've heard music can be helpful," he agreed, his voice kind and soft. 'Harry' was written on his name badge.

He led her over to one of the walls, covered in shelves full of CDs.

"Classical?" he asked, as if he could read her mind. He trailed his finger along the spines. "Something harmonic yet stirring?"

"Oh, yes. Whatever you think." Olivia noted that his fingernails were well kept, not torn and abused like hers.

With thick, blunt fingers, he pulled out a selection of six

CD cases. Not the fingers of a musician, but someone who appreciated music judging by his familiarity with the titles.

"I hope these help." He handed them over with a gentle smile. "Don't worry, I'll register them with the hospital's account. Bring them back whenever you'd like to change them."

"Thank you," Olivia managed to say, struggling to control her sudden tears. His kindness made her want to pour out all her fears, to feel comforting arms enfold her.

"Will you come back and tell me how it goes?" he asked, his expression full of understanding.

"Sure," Olivia said, knowing she would likely drop the CDs back via the return chute. He threatened her fragile control, and she couldn't bear to think ahead to a point where she would be finished with them. "Thank you, Harry," she whispered to his retreating back.

At the hospital, Olivia played through the selection of CDs from the library. Harry knew his music, his selection soothing yet uplifting, the violins sweet, not mournful. She glanced at Jessie and her gaze sharpened. There seemed to be a hint of color in her cheeks, and unless she was imagining it, the expression on her sister's beautiful face was more serene than she'd ever seen.

THE COMPOSER

LONDON 1913

Archibald wakes late, groggy from the effects of the opium. Despite the lingering sense of unreality, he feels alive, all his senses heightened. By the teasing aroma of fresh bread, he knows the day maid has been. He makes a pot of tea and butters some bread, taking sustenance for the day, eating with enthusiasm for the first time in an age.

He will finish the symphony today.

It is clear in his mind, although not quite complete, cut off like the kiss that never eventuated, but he is close. Then he will find her, his muse. Will she come to him lively in pale blue, or solemn and pale in midnight and gold?

The thought of her presence gives him the strength to return to his old school, where he *will* finish. It *will* be the best piece he has ever composed.

And finish he does, his triumph flowing from his heart to the piano, from his fingers through the conduit of ink onto the paper. With the music she showed him, he scribbles in the intrinsic harmony of the koto, the overlay of the Japanese flute. Excitement pulses through him. The instruments from the exhibition are still in London. It will be up to the conductor to find musicians to play them.

He writes the last notes with a flourish, a sense of relief so overwhelming he feels weightless. By creating such a beautiful piece of music, he has ensured immortality for his son. The orchestra will have time to perfect their performance before opening night.

He has not let Benjamin down.

Locking the sheet music in the safe, Archibald tells himself he will return and make a good copy tomorrow. For now, he just wants to walk the streets and float on the ecstasy of his achievement. Savor his triumph—and look for her.

Breathing the frigid night air, he strolls with the surety that he has written a piece of music which will live on beyond his lifetime. Music that will be heard by generations to come, in honor of his son. Just hearing the echoes of the flute in his head as he makes his way home warms his soul, his step lighter than it has been since his first heady realization that he could communicate his emotions and creativity through music.

He pulls the old coin out of his waistcoat pocket, willing her to appear.

In the fading dusk, the faintest flash of blue catches his eye. His steps quicken as he hurries to keep up. She waits for him until he is almost close enough to touch her, then moves away, looking over her shoulder, smiling at him. He laughs, and feeling playful, breaks into a jog.

He imagines the feel of her in his arms, her kiss in the swoop and soar of the music he has just finished. He knows as surely as there is breath in his lungs that they will be together. His calves begin to burn. He sucks in gulps of fresh Greenwich air.

Air scented with jasmine.

An opaque veil drops from his vision. He knows her. *Remembers* her.

"Mayumi," he calls out to the woman draped in pale blue.

He can be with her now.

She stops, waiting for him, glowing in the dim night.

Just a little farther...

She turns to face him. She is close now. He can see that it is not a dress she wears but a formless garment like a sack. Clutched against her chest is a gray, furry object. It is an animal, but not one he has never seen before. Some kind of small bear?

He looks up to her face and realizes she is not Mayumi of the red lips, but the apparition he first saw in his studio at the school. The woman with lively brown eyes. Her lovely face promising the tranquility he craves.

Her name comes to him on the perfumed air.

"Jasmine," he whispers, reaching for her, but all he feels are the silken threads of her hair against his fingers before she is gone.

He throws himself forward, desperate not to lose her. He is flying, falling, the water welcoming him, soaking his clothes, dragging him under. He smiles, sinking into her embrace.

THE MUSE'S SISTER

LONDON 1998

Olivia made her way from the hospital through the darkening London streets, her steps weighted with failure she wasn't ready to acknowledge. Another day at her sister's bedside would be followed by another night crying herself to sleep in the tiny studio apartment she'd rented.

For lack of anything more productive to do, and for a change from hastily steamed vegetables and rice, she stopped by the supermarket to buy the ingredients to make her sister's favorite dish. Although the key ingredient eluded her at first, she persisted and returned to her room with a bag of groceries—including a jar of Vegemite.

The taste of Jessie's favorite comfort food took Olivia back to their childhood on the farm—the sound of Jessie learning to play the violin, hot summer days swimming in the waterhole. She could almost feel the comfort of her sister's arms around her, telling her everything would be fine.

The next day Olivia carried a bowl of pasta to the hospital with her, and asked the nurse if she would organize for it to be warmed up, with the desperate hope the smell would rouse Jessie.

Like every day the last week, Olivia spent the morning reading out loud from her notebook of their childhood memories with CDs from the library playing in the background. How long would they follow this routine before there was a change?

She had been back to the library twice to ask Harry's advice for new music to play for her sister, her appreciation for the music and her new friend growing. It was easy to picture him listening to the music he'd recommended with a relaxed smile on his face. Olivia could imagine listening to it with him, standing together on a balcony on a warm night, close but not quite touching. Drinking wine and looking at the stars and sharing stories of the things they loved best about their childhoods. Talking about the people who mattered to them.

A slow tear meandered down her cheek. *So tired.* Resting her head on her sister's thigh, she let the music pull her down, tugging her to a soft place where there was no worry or pain.

Olivia woke with a start. Had Jessie moved? Or spoken?

She looked up at her sister's face and was surprised to find her looking back, her eyes wide and clear, her mouth curved into a soft smile. "I love you, Livvy. Thank you for keeping me company and for introducing me to Archibald.

Remember, I will always be with you. Please, don't be sad. I am where I'm supposed to be."

A hand on her shoulder startled Olivia, wrenching her from sleep. Monitors were screeching. Glancing back at her sister's face, she was shocked to find it so changed, slack, her head drooped to one side, skin clammy and the color of a pale gray pearl. The head of her toy koala rested in her open palm.

"What's happening?" Olivia asked, confused, panicking. She'd just spoken to her sister, hadn't she? She'd just looked healthy and full of life.

"I'm sorry love, but if you're going to stay, you need to step back," the nurse said, hurriedly helping her to her feet and steering her away from the bed.

The doctor bustled in, checked the monitors and inspected her sister. He turned to Olivia with a look of concern.

Olivia was confused. What was going on?

"Miss Thompson? I'm sorry, but as you know there was very little hope your sister would wake. I have put off bringing up the topic of turning off the life support, but it looks like your sister has made her own decision. This happens sometimes." He placed a tentative hand on her shoulder. "I hope it brings you some consolation to know that she was at peace. She had you with her at the end. We'll give you some time alone."

The doctor and nurse left the room and closed the door.

Stunned, empty and numb, Olivia sat on the edge of the bed and took Jessie's hand. She couldn't be gone. The hand in hers was limp, as it had been since she'd been here, but different.

A wrenching sob rose in Olivia. Her sister lay next to her, but her lifeforce was gone.

After a night of sleeping-tablet-induced sleep, Olivia took her usual path to the hospital, still numb with shock. She said goodbye to the nurses and collected the bag of Jessie's belongings along with her CD player and the CDs. She didn't remember catching the train or walking, but found herself back at her temporary apartment.

As she warmed up the rest of the Vegemite mac and cheese, she set the table for two and put on the CD that was in the player when Jessie died.

She ate with tears running down her face. They splashed into her bowl, onto the pasta she spooned into her mouth. The symphony played on and gradually her tears slowed, the music soothing her, bringing a feeling of peace. After dinner, Olivia cleaned up. Jessie *had* spoken to her before she'd left. And at least if she was gone, she was at peace. She would have wanted Olivia to remember her for the good times, not be sad.

With a determination that helped her to look forward, she decided to buy a copy of the CD to take home, so she could play it to feel close to her sister and remember that they had been together at the end.

Clutching the medallion the nurse said Jessie had in her

hand when the ambulance brought her in, Olivia sat down with the CD and her notepad and pen. She pulled out the insert from the case. *A collection of the last works of Archibald Flagstaff, including a symphony completed before his suspected suicide by drowning, Greenwich 1913, at the height of his creativity.*

Ironic that he had drowned close to where Jessie had her accident.

In her notebook, Olivia wrote: *composer—Archibald Flagstaff.* A memory tugged at her. Archibald? Hadn't her sister mentioned that name? At the end?

Olivia pressed *play* on her Discman and scrolled through to the piece that was playing when Jessie passed. The second to last track on the CD—the fourth movement of *The Ways of Life.* Olivia stared at the list of music titles, then out the window at the gray sky outside. Her mind raced. *It couldn't be.* She looked back at the list and shook her head, a soft smile growing.

The title of the movement was *'Crépuscule de Jasmine'.* Twilight of Jasmine.

Olivia heard Jessie's last words again in her mind, spoken from spirit to spirit. *"I am where I'm supposed to be."*

The next day Olivia went to the library to return the CDs. In person.

Although fighting to contain her pain and desolation, she felt she had to do this one thing before she packed to go back to Australia. She had promised Harry she would let him know.

He took one look at her and led her to a study nook, away from the curious glances of the staff and patrons. "Olivia. I'm so sorry."

The memory of his earlier kindness broke her reserve and made it possible for her to step into his open arms. His masculine yet soft scent enfolded her, and she lay her cheek against his chest. The already low sounds of the library faded, the solidity of his body after having no-one to hold provided comfort she so desperately needed. His arms wrapped gently around her shoulders and he stood still and let her sob, his cheek resting lightly on the top of her head. In his arms, something that was hard and tight inside loosened. As if something had passed physically from his body to hers, she felt strong enough to go on. She might even be strong enough to stay in London for a while longer.

Olivia stepped back and wiped her eyes.

Pulling a travel pack of tissues from his pocket, Harry offered her one.

After wiping her nose and her eyes, she looked up at him. His gaze caught hers, a sanctuary of warmth and understanding.

"How did you know? Or do you always carry a pack of emergency tissues in your pocket?" She hiccupped a laugh. "Do you often have people crying in the library?"

Harry smiled gently and shrugged. "A feeling I guess."

"Want to know something strange?" She sniffed and attempted a light tone. Without waiting for him to answer, she continued. "Of the CDs you gave me, this was her favorite." Lifting the top case, she turned it to show him the back. "My sister's name is Jasmine."

His expression was knowing, not surprised. "Do you believe in fate?" he asked, his gaze gently probing hers, his voice unlocking defenses she'd held as long as she could remember.

Did she? How could she not, after everything that had happened since she'd arrived in London?

Harry smiled gently. It seemed he'd read her answer in her expression. "She was very lucky to have you as her sister. She's at peace now. Where she is supposed to be."

How could he have known that was the last thing Jasmine had said to her?

"Thank you, Harry. For everything."

PART III

SOULMATES

AYUMI

PARIS 2029

B*athroom, then caffeine.*
The queue for border control snaked out in front and behind Ayumi. She'd arrived at the station late and had foregone a visit to the ladies' room before joining the queue, scared she'd miss the train to London. She couldn't risk missing the last rehearsal before opening night.

She fidgeted from foot to foot, glancing up from checking her messages every few seconds. At least the queue was moving quickly. In no time she was next.

The guy behind the plexiglass waved her forward and took her passport without looking up. Ayumi studied his straight dark brows and perfectly proportioned nose, willing him to let her through quickly.

"You're Australian, with a visa to work in Britain. What were you doing in Paris?" he asked, his tone business-like and weary.

"Visiting a friend," Ayumi said and shifted her weight, her

need for the loo becoming more urgent. "I've settled into lodgings in London, but my job hasn't started yet."

The border control officer looked up, his blue eyes locking on hers for an instant before dropping back to her passport.

Ayumi took a deep breath to calm her sudden jump of nerves. What was it about having your identity checked that made one nervous? Or was it the shock of connection when his eyes had caught and held hers…and the strange feeling of déjà vu?

"My mother is Japanese," she explained, in case her appearance prompted a deeper probe into her identity. 'Australian' wasn't the first assumption people normally made when they first saw her.

But she needn't have bothered. He'd already stamped her passport and handed it back under the gap in the screen, a slight frown on his face. His eyes locked with hers again, then he released her passport with a smile that warmed his stern expression—and made him very attractive.

"Glad to have you in London."

Ayumi glanced down at his name badge, wanting to thank him by name, but there was only a number. "Thanks," she said, and meant it. After only a few days, London felt like a second home. As pleasant as her visit to Paris had been, she was happy to return to the other side of the Channel.

With a relieved smile, she hurried to find the nearest bathroom–after a quick glance back at his booth. Through the door she could make out a slim waist and wide shoulders accentuated by his navy uniform, his dark blonde hair cut short to reveal a glimpse of his toned and tanned neck.

Ayumi sighed, frustrated. It was just her luck to meet a cute guy when there was no time to get to know him.

Ten minutes later, Ayumi perched on the only available chair in the only café on the concourse, sipping her *café allongé* as though her life depended on it. The caffeine wasn't quite *that* important, but she did need to stay awake for the two-hour trip to London. She had a symphony to perform. After days without practicing and staying up too late last night, she needed to brush up on the score.

The quick trip to Paris had been worth it though. She hadn't seen Bridgette since they'd studied together in New York, and two days had not been long enough to catch up on what had happened since. So many jobs and new cities for them both—and new men, in Bridgette's case. Her friend never had shown the same commitment to her career as Ayumi.

She glanced up from the email she was trying to phrase politely, asking again for the organizers to correct her name on the tour website. The large clock on the wall said ten minutes until she could board. Ten minutes until she could get settled and concentrate. Until then she could enjoy this last glimpse of France. She glanced around the crowd, who seemed to be either British businesspeople or French families heading to London for the weekend.

Her gaze caught on the man in uniform walking quickly

past the café, his dark blonde head swiveling as he scanned the crowded concourse. Ayumi recognized him as the attractive officer who had processed her passport. She stiffened, wondering if he might be looking for someone who had slipped through the screening process. She hoped whatever it was wouldn't delay the train—she was already cutting it fine.

She watched him as he searched, admiring the way his uniform fit his athletic physique to perfection. She turned and tilted her head to study him in more detail. His posture and movements conveyed confidence, without the pushiness of arrogance. He really was very attractive, even when he frowned.

What if they met here again, when she next visited Bridgette? Would he recognize her? Give her that same soft smile?

He was close now, and she could see him clearly through the café patrons. He turned—and his face lit up.

"Ms. Ambrose," he called and wove through the crowd to her table.

Ayumi frowned. Had she dropped something at the counter? Her international credit card?

"Can I help you?" she asked when he stopped in front of her.

"I need to get back to my booth, but I was hoping…that is, could we catch up in London? My next day off is Sunday. Think about it. As soon as all the passengers are processed, I could come and see you on the train…before you leave?"

Ayumi felt giddy at the thought he had especially come to

find her. He'd sought her out because he wanted to talk to her, to see her. "Oh! Yes." Ayumi's smile wavered. Sunday she had a show *and* a matinee. "Except..."

"Which carriage are you in, and which seat?" he said hurriedly, glancing over his shoulder as if worried he'd be missed.

Ayumi scrambled for the boarding pass in her handbag, but he was already stepping away, an anxious yet eager expression on his face. What had he risked to find her? A reprimand? His job?

"Ah. Carriage six, seat 4D," she called out with a smile to show him she was aware of the trouble he'd taken to find her.

He waved, his blue eyes crinkling at the corners with the size of his grin. Then he was gone, jogging away.

Ayumi picked up her cup, excitement bubbling in her stomach, so many thoughts dashing through her mind. Would they be able to organize a time to meet? Was she wrong, or was what just happened terribly romantic?

A date! It wouldn't be such a big deal for most other women. If one wasn't constantly moving around for work a relationship didn't pose a serious logistical challenge. If Ayumi ever found someone she wanted to get to know better, the best she could hope for was a few dates before she had to move on. This tour was a little different though—a whole six weeks in Britain, with many of the venues in or not far from London. Even the far-flung locations in Scotland weren't as much of a trek as when she worked in Australia, or the time she'd toured the US.

She didn't know anything about the handsome border control officer, but she was sure she hadn't mistaken the mutual attraction between her and...*she didn't even know his name!*

Passengers were still streaming through passport control when the boarding call came. Agitated with excitement, Ayumi wheeled her carry-on case toward the platform for the train to London and pulled out her boarding pass. Carriage four, seat 6D. She stepped into the air-conditioned carriage and made her way down the aisle until she found row 6, took out her laptop, and stowed her case.

Scooting over to the window, she glanced out, anticipation fluttering in her stomach. With trembling hands, she opened her laptop and plugged it in to charge, her head snapping up at the sound of the final boarding call. As she scanned the people moving through the carriage, Ayumi was surprised at how intensely she wanted to see him again. *Would her mystery man find her before the train left?*

She didn't know his name or have any way of contacting him. Her next visit to Paris wouldn't be until the tour was over, when there would be no reason for her to stay in London. And the chance of him being on duty when she did was slim. If the train pulled away without her seeing him, they might never meet again!

Damn. He must have been too busy to come find her—or maybe he'd forgotten. Her daydream of getting to know him and the excitement of a possible romance faded as quickly as it had flared to life. Ayumi took a swig of bottled water to dilute the taste of disappointment.

Her stomach clenched as the doors slid closed. The departure announcement began to cycle through multiple languages. Still no sign of him.

She knelt on the seat, looking out the window as the doors slid closed. Ayumi cursed herself for not stepping out of the carriage for a moment to look for him. It was too late now...

On the almost deserted platform, a figure dressed in navy burst from the train two carriages back. Carriage six. *The one she had told him she was in.*

Shit, shit, shit. She'd mixed up the seat number with the carriage number!

The train began to move as he jogged in her direction. For a moment he pulled level with her carriage.

Pressing her hand against the window, she mouthed the word 'sorry', but she couldn't be sure he had seen her through the glass. Despair filled her as his jog slowed and the train pulled away.

They'd only shared a few words, but in that short time she'd felt a connection she'd never experienced with anyone she'd just met. Ayumi sat back in her seat, surprised to find herself blinking back tears as the train picked up speed, too quickly taking her farther from him...

ARCHIE

LONDON 2029

For the rest of his shift, Archie struggled to focus on his work, his thoughts on the beguiling woman with the vibrant brown eyes who had drifted through his world and turned it upside down, leaving a scent of jasmine in her wake. The thought of spending time with her and getting to know her had been like a flash of sunlight on a dull autumn day.

He had to restrain himself from logging in to access the manifest to search for Ayumi Ambrose and her contact details. He had already severely broken protocol by closing his booth to look for her.

Maybe she didn't want to talk to him or see him again but was too polite to tell him straight out. Maybe she'd given him the wrong carriage on purpose, so he didn't find her.

It stung more than a simple rejection should have, the connection he thought they'd made like nothing he'd felt before. As if they'd known each other somehow, although he would have remembered if he'd met her, even in passing.

More than her beauty and quiet grace, she had piqued his interest as no woman ever had. With a smile and a few soft-spoken words, she had brightened his day. It was as if fate had brought them together. Except she hadn't, had she? Archie rubbed his chest to try to ease the tight, heavy feeling there. Cruel fate had teased him with a glimpse of possibility, then torn it away.

A four-day stint in France had never felt so long, but eventually Sunday came around and he returned to London with the promise of good weather for his days off. Even the blue skies couldn't break his melancholy mood though.

After visiting his Canary Wharf flat to unpack and put a load of washing on, Archie aimlessly wandered along the Thames. With the comforting weight of his aunt's medallion in his pocket, he watched the river traffic and people as if Ayumi might magically appear. He had resisted the urge to search for her online. If she had deliberately thrown him off the scent, he would not stalk her. Even so, he couldn't help feeling frustrated and helpless. Here he was in the same city she was—but he had no idea where. She said she was working. What did she do? And how long would she be in London for?

He shook his head at himself. He *was* becoming a stalker. He just really wanted to see her again. He ran his hand through his hair, grasping the warm strands at the back of his neck and tugging. Damn it, he had to find her, just in case it *had* been a legitimate mistake. What if she went back to Australia next week and was gone forever?

He released his hair and straightened his shoulders. He would do whatever he could to find her. Pulling out his phone he searched her name on the internet.

Ayumi Ambrose came up with nothing but a private Facebook profile, with a generic picture of a Japanese bridge and cherry blossom tree. His finger hovered over 'friend request'. He took a bracing breath—and pressed it. If she didn't reply, or it wasn't her, when he was back at work on Wednesday he would log in to the manifest from last Friday. There would have to be a phone number or email address where he could contact her. Even if she thought it was creepy, he'd rather risk it than miss this chance. He wanted to trust his gut so much he would risk his job.

Feeling a little better for having a plan, Archie stopped on the path by the river and turned to lean back on the rail, enjoying the holiday feel of salt-laden warm air and the gulls wheeling above him. With the pleasant warmth of the sun on his face, he slitted his eyes and gazed across the green space to an historic building in the distance. It reminded him of the summer he'd volunteered at the library his dad worked at. Each day he'd watched as they passed by in the bus as the old music school building was gutted, ready to be renovated for its new life as a community hall.

Wondering what it was like inside, Archie pushed away from the rail and walked over for a closer look. A canvas banner hung across the top floor, bright against the red brick facade. A symphony, playing for the next week.

Sunday was the day of his regular dinner with his sister, her fortnightly excuse to get out of the house. He'd hoped to be going on a date with Ayumi tonight. Eve would have understood, been thrilled in fact, if he'd called her to say he was ditching her for a date with an Australian girl. Instead, Eve would have to sit through a meal with her grumpy brother.

As he approached the entrance doors, reminiscent of a vintage cinema, Archie took out his phone again and typed a text to his dad, who loved classical music. *Thinking of getting tickets to a symphony at Flagstaff community hall Mon or Tues night. Interested?*

He tried all the doors, thinking he would ask about availability, but they were all locked.

After dinner, Archie headed back to his tiny Canary Wharf apartment on foot and found himself heading in the direction of the river again. Eve had left early after the sitter called to say she wasn't feeling well just as their mains arrived. Sis had taken a doggy bag and left him to finish his steak and glass of wine alone.

He wasn't sure how he had offended Karma, but he was having rotten luck with women—he couldn't even manage a meal with his sister. Poor Eve, she'd been so disappointed. He would call by her Kensington apartment the next day with flowers to cheer her up and say hi to the tadpole.

Archie thought about contacting any one of his mates he knew would be up for a few drinks at the pub, but he didn't feel much likely talking about soccer or property investment.

Instead, he ambled along, watching the flickering reflections on the river as he walked, the uplifting sound of music floating to him on the warm breeze.

The skin on his forearms prickled, the hairs on the back of his neck standing up. *The orchestra at the community hall.* Turning his steps to cross the park, Archie followed the music. Maybe he would be able to buy tickets, for three. Even Mum had been keen to come along, Dad had said with a laugh when he'd called back.

Archie wandered through the entry doors, breathing in the history of the restored building as he scanned the lobby, but there was not a soul around. No-one at the desk or at the temporary bar to ask about tickets. Archie checked his watch. According to the banner, the concert started half an hour ago.

Instead of turning around to leave, his feet carried him deeper inside, drawn by the sweet call of the violin. The notes resonated with something deep inside him, like a forgotten melody from childhood. With every step, the music grew in intensity, circling him, weaving a spell around him, drawing him deeper.

Archie paused. All the doors to the auditorium were closed—except one, a small side door. He followed the now-haunting melody to the door and the music seemed to reach out and wrap around him, binding him, so he couldn't turn back, even if he wanted to. Even if security told him to. It felt as if was meant to be here, that somehow the decisions of his life had led him here, to this night. This place.

Holding his breath, he entered the auditorium, stepping

sideways so he was hidden in the shadows, his back against the wall. Taking shallow breaths, Archie was unable to move or take his gaze from the stage, a vortex of sound and movement in contrast to the silent stillness of the audience.

Amidst the small orchestra, he picked out the violins, the source of the resonance in his chest.

It was almost too much for his senses. For a moment, he closed his eyes to focus on the emotion of the music. With his eyes closed, he picked out an unexpected sound–a haunting drift of mist, the flight of a crane–high over the other instruments. A Japanese flute, wailing with the pain of loss.

Archie opened his eyes, but instead of finding the flutist, he found his vision funneled to the dark-haired young woman playing lead violin. Even sitting, her lithe figure and the grace of her movements were unmistakable. Shock and relief hit him like a shove to the chest.

Ayumi!

The sound of the flute subsided and his heart soared, higher than the triumphant rise of the strings. He'd found her! In the immense population of London, the music had drawn him to her.

She was radiant. Beautiful. With her eyes closed, she lived the music. The expressions on her face reflected the shifting moods of the piece, from foreboding to pain, from tentative joy to elation.

AYUMI

LONDON 2029

Being able to lose herself in a perfectly executed piece of music was the one thing she loved most about performing. The feeling of being transported to another place and time, whilst still being intimately connected to the emotions of the audience. Only a loud noise, an off-note, or a particularly emotive response in the audience could penetrate her sanctuary.

In that moment, *something* did.

Ayumi looked around the auditorium, searching faces illuminated by the soft glow from the stage lighting. She wanted to see the expression of epiphany. It was her reward for sacrifices made and extended periods away from home.

As the composition approached the crescendo, her gaze lifted to the figures at the back of the audience, to a man standing in the shadows. She could not see him clearly, but she had a sense she knew him.

By the angle of his head and the glint of his eyes she could tell he was looking directly at her. The intensity of attention gave the impression he was there for her. *He had been searching for her.* For the first time since she began performing, it was *she* that experienced the epiphany. She *knew* him. Knew that her mystery man had found her.

Their gazes locked. With the sweet and satisfying feeling of a string tuned to perfect pitch, she completed the final movement of the symphony with the orchestra. She played through the encore, stood and bowed through the applause, then packed her violin in its case, impatient for the others to leave, chatting and fussing over plans to meet for a quick drink to wind down. She didn't need to look to know that he was there. She could *feel* him.

Her heart fluttered as the stage lights flicked off one by one, then stuttered as the auditorium fell silent.

Leaving her violin case next to her chair, she stepped down from the stage then headed for the stairs that would take her to the tiered seating.

"Hello again," she whispered, knowing the acoustics would carry her voice to where she sensed him waiting.

"About that date..." he said, as if resuming a conversation they'd merely paused. His deep voice reached out to her through the dimness, teasing with a hint of uncertainty.

"I'm sorry." He *had* wondered if she switched the numbers on purpose. She'd regretted her error multiple times every day since she'd missed him on the platform in Paris. "It was a mistake. I should have checked..."

"That's okay. Luckily our paths have crossed again." His voice dipped, "I could ask you out now."

"Or I could ask you." She managed a teasing tone that belied her racing heart. "Would you like to join me for a drink? There's a bar not far from here."

"I'd love to," he said, stepping out of the shadows into the row lighting, the shadow of a promise unfurling with his silhouette.

"Great. I just need to store my violin and grab my bag."

"I'll wait," he said, his voice low, promising more than the immediate future. More than this one night, more than a casual drink. It promised a future of companionship and passion.

Ayumi didn't want to wait. She wanted it all. Now. She didn't want to waste a single moment, or risk losing him again. She wanted to throw her arms around him and cry with relief that they'd found each other.

"Shall we meet outside in the foyer?" she asked.

"There is only one?" His frown made her stomach flutter. He didn't want to lose her again either.

"Yes," she smiled. "We won't miss each other this time."

Ayumi turned and hurried to lock her instrument away and retrieve the lucky plectra she'd found at a flea market the first time she'd visited London. She slipped the three bone finger picks into the pocket of her dress. She didn't pause to check her lipstick or straighten her hair. Deep down she knew it didn't matter. She just wanted to be near him and learn everything about him.

ARCHIE

"You know, I still don't know your name." Ayumi's low, sensual voice reached out from behind the column at his back. He'd been waiting, standing by a high table in a daze, two glasses by his hand.

"How rude of me!" He turned to her, flustered. Had he really not introduced himself? "Sorry. For some reason, I thought you knew."

"No don't tell me," she said and held up her hand. Tilting her head playfully, her gaze searched his face. "Theodore?" She giggled, sweet as the tinkling of a small bell.

"Really?" He smiled, then, remembering the drinks, turned to pick them up. "I hope you like champagne. I thought I'd get us a drink here so we can talk. In case the jazz bar is too loud."

"You read my mind," Ayumi smiled and took the glass he offered. "Give me a minute and I'll see if I can read yours." With a raised eyebrow she lifted her glass.

"To getting to know each other," he ventured and picked up his drink, his gaze caught by her sparkling eyes.

"To getting to know each other well," she said and touched the lip of her glass with his. She took a sip, still studying him. "Something beginning with 'A?'"

"You do know! But we don't wear name badges on duty. Only identifying numbers for security."

"I don't know. Truly. It was a guess." Ayumi straightened and looked deep into his eyes. "I'm getting Archibald, but that name doesn't suit you."

"Now I know you're kidding," he sputtered and put his glass down before he spilled it. It couldn't possibly be a coincidence.

"What do you mean?" Ayumi pulled back a little, looking a little hurt.

Instinctively he reached out to her, placing his hand over hers on the table. A charge from where their fingers touched flared over his skin. His eyes flew to meet hers.

She gazed, wide-eyed, back at him.

She'd felt it too.

He took a steadying breath. "My mother called me Archibald. It was the name her sister whispered when she died after a boating accident. She was Australian, you know." He shut his mouth, aware he was babbling. "The name didn't stick. Everyone calls me Archie."

"Oh my god, I got it right?" Ayumi laughed, turning her hand beneath his so their palms touched. She lifted his hand and shook it. "Very nice to meet you, Archie." She leaned forward, lips parted. "I like it."

The lights dimmed, the signal for the last stragglers to leave the hall so they could close up.

Archie panicked, holding onto her hand, not ready to say good-bye now he'd found her.

"We can still go to that bar I mentioned," she suggested, turning her hand in his and leading him to the door.

Archie's heart swelled with joy. *She felt the same.*

AYUMI

"Actually, I have a better idea." Ayumi rarely drank alcohol after a performance. Even the one glass of champagne had softened her senses, when she most wanted to be fully aware of every moment as it passed. "There's something I do to help me relax after a performance. You could join me…"

While most of the other musicians went in search of a pub to share their post-performance buzz, she'd found a better way to savor hers, easing the adrenalin from her body with the familiarity of ritual. It was a very personal act, but why dance around getting to know each other? Why not invite him to share one of the more intimate aspects of her life?

"Whatever it is, I'd love to," he said, his eyes sparkling with amusement. "I'm in your hands."

Ayumi blushed at the thought of what else would relax her, glad of the shadows that hid her reaction. She'd often yearned for a long and passionate lovemaking session after a particularly stirring performance, but never had the opportunity to create a *new* ritual.

Despite the temptation to take him to her room, she led a silent Archie through the maze of historic alleyways, his large hand warm in hers. She stopped in front of a slatted cedar door and swung it open for him to enter, then followed him into the courtyard of a small Japanese restaurant. Rather than continue to the entrance, she veered off and led the way to a timber teahouse lit by translucent paper lanterns, the familiar crunch of gravel beneath her boots and the tinkle of water unwinding the first coil of performance tension.

Shimmering reflections from lights in the pond illuminated their way up the steps.

Ayumi knelt on the cushion at the head of the low table and waited for Archie to sit opposite. She glanced at him before taking up the instruments that were left for her at the same time every night that she performed.

He watched her, at once trusting and curious. She felt the caress of his gaze as she followed each calming step of the ritual that connected her to ancestors. Her heart slowed, adrenalin dispersing as a haze of pleasurable fatigue washed through her body. Each breath past her lips felt like a prayer to the god who had granted her the talent to create music to the highest standards. Sometimes it felt as if she were possessed. By musicians past or her ancestors, she couldn't be sure. Whomever it was, she was glad to share the spotlight and the experience with them. She never felt alone when she cradled her violin against her cheek and her soul exuded music.

When the first cup of tea was made, she handed the glazed earthenware cup across the table, bowing her head as Archie accepted the foaming tea with both hands and a solemn expression.

"This is matcha, a powdered green tea used in Japanese tea ceremonies," she explained. "A full ceremony can take up to four hours. Mine is the condensed version, but it is enough to help me find tranquility after the excitement of performing."

She then made her own cup. Together, they sipped. With her eyes locked on Archie's, which held a slightly bewildered expression, she exhaled the last coil of tension from her body.

ARCHIE

Archie had never had an occasion to witness a tea ceremony or drink Japanese tea. The first taste was a revelation.

In a daze, caught somewhere between the courtyard of a Japanese restaurant in the middle of London and a world inside his soul he had not known existed, he drank with her. *Ayumi.* The woman he'd yearned to find since they'd met only days earlier. Or had it been longer? *So much longer.*

When his cup was drained, he placed it carefully on the table. The bitter, refreshing aftertaste of the tea lingered on his tongue, foreign yet comfortingly familiar, like a memory from an unknown and unexpected past that reached out to him. He closed his eyes, straining to grasp the memories that swirled just out of reach.

Haunting music drifted on a gust of salt-laden air. Against his eyelids Archie saw patterns of ivory and gold and midnight blue. Tranquility stole through his body and he opened his eyes, expecting to find the beautiful, petite woman he'd met in Paris, the violin player who had bewitched an entire audience with her passionate performance.

He found Ayumi before him, ethereal as a dream, her glossy dark hair now arranged in a more intricate style than before. He squinted. His eyes were playing tricks on him. Her rosebud mouth, which had blushed pink against the healthy glow of her face, flashed scarlet against ghostly white. Her eyes, deepest brown and fringed with lush dark lashes, flared crimson at the corners like the most exotic of butterflies.

He blinked and the make-up was gone. A pale woman sat before him, in a blue hospital gown, her hair no longer bound but loose around her face. Her lips curved in a smile of recognition and joy.

She stood, and in one fluid movement, her form solidified. She was again the Ayumi he knew, dressed in a figure-hugging navy dress.

With a graceful movement of her arm, she held out her hand to him.

REUNION

"Thank you for walking me home," Ayumi said, the silky lining of Archie's jacket like a warm caress against her bare arms. The night had turned cool and she'd forgotten her wrap in her haste to be with him. She felt like she was floating, anchored by his warm hand wrapped around hers, adrenalin dispersed to a hazy buzz of fatigued post-performance pleasure all through her body, more intense than usual in his presence.

His scent enfolded her, yet he was still too far away.

"Thank *you* for the tea. And I'm extremely glad to be able to walk with you at all." He squeezed her hand lightly, sending a thrill of anticipation through her body. "Especially as I'll know where you are next time you give me the slip," he chuckled, hesitant.

She was also glad he would know where to find her when she was performing in London; that is, when he wasn't rostered to work in Paris. He'd been so understanding about her mistake. It could have cost them so dearly—this night, and whatever lay in their future.

"So, your mother is Australian," she asked him. "Is that why you gave me the fifth degree in Paris?"

"I admit it did jolt me out of automatic pilot, although once I looked into your eyes, I knew I had to see you again." His admission, delivered in a low tone, stirred a flurry of butterflies in her belly.

"Was your mum backpacking when she and your father met? Or was he?" The typical holiday romance turned love-of-a-lifetime?

"Actually, her adopted sister was a musician. Coincidentally, also a violinist. She was touring here when she had an accident and Mum came over to be with her. Their parents weren't up to the trip. They're both gone now, so Dad, my sister, and I are all the family Mum has."

A shiver fluttered over Ayumi, her skin puckering as if a cold draft had found her. "Her sister died?" Seeking warmth and comfort, she slid her free hand into Archie's jacket pocket.

"Yes. Dad was working in the library not far from the hospital when Mum went in to borrow some CDs to play for her sister. Aunt Jasmine was in a coma, and the nurses suggested music might help bring her back."

"But it didn't?"

"No," he said and slowed, looking wistful. "I wish I'd known her. She was pretty special. I suppose I have her to thank for being here at all. If it wasn't for her accident, my parents may never have met."

"Fate," Ayumi whispered and stopped walking, her fingers finding the uneven edge of a round, metallic object. "Do you believe? In fate?"

Archie stopped too and turned to face her, threading his fingers through her other hand. "How can I not, the way we found each other again?" He glanced at the sky, then down at Ayumi's face. "It's strange that my aunt should come up tonight. When I moved out of home Mum gave me a medallion Jasmine had with her when she was admitted to hospital. I carry it with me when I'm in London. It's in the right pocket of my jacket."

"This?" Ayumi asked and pulled her hand from the pocket. She tilted the irregular metal disc, so the streetlight lit its face.

"That's it. My lucky charm. I wish I'd had it in Paris."

They both looked at the medallion, then at each other.

"It's very old and quite stylized, but I can see it's the Greek goddess Psyche." Ayumi tilted it so he could see.

"How can you tell?" He leaned in to study the winged figure.

"I was mad about the Greek myths at school. When I wasn't practicing the violin I was reading. I can tell its Psyche because she carries cakes in each hand. When she was sent by Venus to visit the underworld, she took honeyed barley cakes with her to distract Cerberus, who guarded the entrance."

"What was she sent to the underworld?"

"To collect a dose of beauty from Proserpina, queen of the underworld. She also carried two coins to pay the ferryman—one to enter the underworld, and one to return. Her return is seen as the soul's rebirth and represents reincarnation."

Archie looked up at her, his gaze intense. She wondered what he was thinking. He'd looked at her as if he could see into her very soul ever since she'd shared her tea ceremony with him. In truth, she'd also felt a tangible shift between them.

"I know it sounds forward...We've only just met..." Archie said with a slight frown, "but my mother would love to meet you."

"It doesn't feel like it though, does it? And don't worry, you won't scare me off. I'm sure your mother is lovely, if she's anything like you."

Archie stepped closer and dipped his head to keep eye contact. "You feel it too? This thing between us. I thought I was deluded, feeling as if I already knew you. From the moment I looked into your eyes..."

"Are you always so romantic? How is it you're still single?" Ayumi joked, her eyes dropping to his lips.

"Maybe I'm very discerning," he said, the corners of his mouth tipping up. "Only the right girl will do."

His proximity made Ayumi light-headed. Or maybe she'd just forgotten to breathe. Pulling her hand from his, she rested it on his chest to keep her balance. "I felt it—feel it—too," she said, lifting her gaze to his, her eyes moist with emotion. She felt his shuddering breath beneath her palm.

"I know it's only, well, it's not even really a first date..."

He trailed off, lifting his hand yet stopping before he laid it against her cheek.

"Archie. Please kiss me," she said, her voice tight with the effort of containing her anticipation.

Slowly, he lay his palm against her cheek and lowered his head. The space between them compressed, until his lips hovered, millimeters from hers.

Ayumi ached for the brush of his mouth on hers, but she also wanted to hang on this sweet precipice forever, to savor the anticipation of the moment of their first kiss, the sweet impact of their lips and tongues meeting in the most intimate of communication.

As if by agreement, they waited, sharing matcha-scented sighs. A symphony of breath.

"Psyche represents the rebirth of the soul," Ayumi whispered against his lips. "Her name means 'breath of life.'"

When the attraction could be resisted no longer, lips brushed, parted, and surely yet softly, met.

Their kiss contained not only the heady rush of first contact, but the impact of two souls reconnecting, unlocking forgotten memories. *Her soul recognized his.* Lifetimes of love and loss intertwined, sealing their passion in a covenant of belonging.

With the medallion clenched in her hand, Ayumi remembered her past lives—and his. Lifetimes woven and intertwined as intricately as the most complex symphony.

Ambrose. The Englishman who had tried to free her, a woman in bondage. *A geisha.*

Archibald. The tortured composer, the genius who, with

her help in another incarnation, had created the symphony she'd performed this last week. In that life she had held this very medallion and followed his music beneath the waves of the Thames.

Archie. The man who held her firmly yet gently, as if she were more precious than life itself. The man she loved, kissing her with the passion of three lifetimes.

Finally, they had found a place where they both knew freedom and the promise of the rest of their lives.

Finally, they had found each other, a future together the sweetest reward for the tenacity of their love.

The original spark of this story came to me during meditation.

Many thanks to the lovely Jen for re-introducing me to a beautiful piece of music,
"A Way of Life" by Hans Zimmer.

I wish I had the musical knowledge to
do the piece justice with my words.

Thank you for reading *Symphony of Breath*.
If you enjoyed it, please consider leaving a review wherever you purchased the book.
And take a look at *Island of Lost Flowers*,
a dual timeline novella:
books2read.com/islandoflostflowers

Coming in 2023...

Chameleon: *the many transformations of Henrietta Browne*

A mixed-race woman's struggle to remain free and achieve the success she deserves in a world rife with racial, religious and sexual prejudice during
a time of global upheaval.
From Jazz Age Paris to the Nazi-occupied Champagne region.

Contact Jo via facebook.com/JoEdgarBakerAuthor
Find her books at books2read.com/joedgarbaker
and amazon.com/author/joedgarbaker

March 2025
Lee B. - it is OK.
Not much of a book.

www.ingramcontent.com/pod-product-compliance
Lightning Source LLC
LaVergne TN
LVHW041105230225
804348LV00031B/794